THE
EPIC QUEST
FOR
TERRAL B. HYLOTZ

ANDREW PIKE

Published in Canada by Engen Books, St. John's, NL.

CIP Data for the title is available on the Library and Archives Canada website.

ISBN-13: 978-1-77478-063-3

Distributed by:
Engen Books
www.engenbooks.com
submissions@engenbooks.com

First mass market paperback printing: December 2021
Cover Design: Graham Blair Designs

THE
EPIC QUEST
FOR
TERRAL B. HYLOTZ

ANDREW PIKE

ENGEN
BOOKS

THE
EPIC QUEST
FOR
FERRAL B. HYLOTZ

ANDREW PIKE

Cold
Shivers through snowy forests
Green branches against ashen gusts
Towers high in the distance
Through twilight passage
Warmth of friends?
Waves brighten darkness
Biting mountains forbode death
Beyond many race brilliant stars
Seek home for relief from
The Storm

Dedicated to my dad, Lloyd Pike
And the Engen community, especially readers like you.

Thank you for believing!

PART ONE
EARTH
WITH: FATHOM

I

Light blasted through the windshield with all the terror of a nuclear explosion, and waves of razor-sharp shards of glass rained over me like acid searing my skin. The smell of my blood mixed with the bitter cold of the storm. My arms strained against the ambulance's efforts to veer off its path, swerving left and right like I was dodging moose in some twisted game of frogger. *Had I hit one?*

The ambulance shook violently, its tires leaving the asphalt and rumbling over the rocks at the side of the road. I tried to swerve back, but it was too late. Shrubbery scratched the driver's side window like a monster trying to break in to berate me on my poor choices up to this point. *Had I driven too fast? Was I paying enough attention to the road? Should I have opted for a different career choice? Certainly.*

Trees vaguely appeared through the white of the storm. Hitting one would spell instant death, but I had now become resigned with a self-depreciating calm. It was really no surprise I'd land myself in a position like this. A perfectly reasonable ending to a life spent satiating the never-ending demands of the hospital.

A tree slammed against the side of the ambulance near-ly toppling the whole thing over. Before I had a chance to regain control, the vehicle gained speed. This was it. The worst-case scenario. Nothing in the wilderness first aid books could prepare me for what was about to happen.

The ambulance halted abruptly on some obstruction causing the whole thing to jolt and I became airborne, floating as if gravity had no further interest in holding on to me.

In a surreal clarity of mind, I made peace with the probable reality that this was the end. *You really messed up this time, bud.*

◄

I stirred to the presence of another. No pain. But shock. I opened my eyes to see a whirling snow lifting and drop-ping around me with a chaotic unrest. There was a surreal quiet to it. If it weren't symptomatic of the looming apoca-lypse, it would be almost charming.

Two barren trees appeared through the storm, with-ered and pale, struggling to stay alive in our endless win-ter. A closer look revealed they were connected to a brown snout and two weary eyes. In my paralysis I panicked as if some unseemly tree-headed monster had come to collect my broken body—lunchtime. When the creature let loose a surprisingly haughty snort, I realized I was staring at a moose. Like me, it looked apprehensive and curious; two creatures face to face with the decimation of our planet, with not a clue what to do about it.

"What a state."

The words seemed to come from nowhere. I attempt-ed to move but could not. After a moment of struggling, I passed out.

◢

"Fathom…this is…EMS…come in…over…"

The voice was distant, scratching through a barrier of white noise, barely intelligible. I exerted the muscles in my arm to lift it, but a cold, dull pain spread through me.

"Fathom…come in…over…"

I pushed through the pain and clutched at my radio. I pulled it to my ear. "Roger EMS, this is Fathom."

"Where are you?"

"Ten minutes from the Last Bastion base, near the Ridgeline Forest."

"…numerous reports of moose…keep an eye out…it's like they've got a mind of their own…"

"EMS, there was an accident…"

The radio sputtered with static, then gave out completely. I cursed, tucking it in my camo winter coat.

How did I get to this point? Years of studying the sciences, a residency of pasty hospital walls, belligerent doctors and apathetic nurses, first response, and now doomed to die in a snowbank. Hell, I shouldn't complain, the way the planet was going with this storm, we were all going to perish soon enough anyway.

I tried to sit up but was reminded once again of the crippling pain; my head was pounding. I surveyed the scene. I was waist deep in snow. My forehead hurt. There was blood in the snow. I unzipped my pocket and removed my last resort first aid kit, undoing a bandage and wrapping it around my head.

The ambulance was nowhere to be seen but its droning was barely audible beneath the roar of the storm, dying like the flatline of an ECG. *Had I fallen off a cliff?* I approached the trees of the Ridgeline Forest. Last Bastion must be close. The northern storms had begun to destroy smaller rural communities and remote locations like the base, leading to a full lockdown within cities. A small unfortunate few, including myself, were tasked with the dangerous job of retrieving those without food and bringing them back to the city.

My trek through the forest provided little shelter from the conditions. With whistling winds burning my eyelids, I walked from tree to tree working outward from the cliff towards—what I expected would be— the coast. I can tell you that the journey is not one I'd wish on anyone. The cold chill pained to the bone. It was enough to make you wish for a quick death.

Leaving the forest, the whistling ocean winds hit me like a heart attack. Though my reserves were bolstered at the sight of the base's spotlight that appeared in the distance like a beacon of hope in the storm. I made my way along the shore until coming upon a cliff below the base.

After a short climb I reached a sheltered summit which offered temporary relief from the storm. The moon cast a peaceful glow over the ocean but it was interrupted by spiraling snowy columns stretching up into space. It looked like a giant nebula had engulfed the planet.

The Last Bastion base had been converted from a lighthouse to a research facility to study the storm, but it had been a fruitless endeavor. Scientists had studied the strange cosmic powder on every possible level, but were no closer to unlocking its secrets. The storm just showed up one day, consuming all in its path, and showed no signs of relenting.

I found a path to the base and ascended a stairway to reach a side door. The lights were off. I banged on the door as hard as I could for at least ten minutes, then I slipped into a defeated squat against the side of the building. My mind raced. Without shelter, safe exposure to a Level 3 storm was estimated at two hours, and I had no idea how long I was passed out. I could die right here like this.

Then, the base door abruptly flew open, blasting me with a puff of warm air and sending clusters of snow swirling up into the night. I recalled a childhood memory of returning home to gingerbread cookies in a hot oven. Pleasant, until I was hit by a cloud of noxious cigarette smoke that burnt my lungs and sent me into a coughing fit.

II

"Right. You're the medical response, eh?" The booming male voice struck me as the porch light flicked on. I rubbed my sleeve against my glasses to clear the condensation. "Not in the best shape, are you?"

The man became visible through a hallway of dirty smoke. The place could have been burning down for all I knew. He had glossy slicked-back hair, a trimmed beard and tattoos covering every inch of his skin. He looked mid-twenties, like me, but his eyes bestowed a fiery wisdom beyond his age.

The man squinted at me. "How exactly do you plan on getting us out of here? You look like you just fell off a cliff." He pulled a cigarette from his mouth and laid a mop against the wall.

"Uhm, yes. I did. My ambulance fell over a cliff. There

was a crash. I don't know what hit me." I stepped inside and closed the door taking a moment to orient myself.

"You sure weren't hit with good looks," he said, bursting into a throaty laughter. "I'm Aaron Myles. Janitorial Apprentice, level fifty-two. You?"

"Jacob Fathom."

"Fathom. Can't imagine a name like that."

"Uhm, well…"

"Come to think of it, knew a guy with that name back at West End Cleaners. Absolute wreck he was, couldn't keep a job, multiple divorces, had some wild out-there stories about the universe though. Musta been the drugs. Never could figure out what he was on about. But the man *could* fix a dishwasher."

I suffered another coughing fit.

"Right, sorry about all the smoke. Government recently reversed no-smoking laws in public facilities, result of the death storm of course. Guess they figured everyone's gonna die anyway, might as well smoke 'em if you got 'em." He took a long draw on his cigarette and exhaled in my general direction, as if he hadn't just then apologized for exactly that. "Between you an' me, they're just in the pocket of smoke companies, right?"

"Sure. Well, we should probably speak to security if we're going to get out of here."

"Right. Let's go for a little walk."

I followed him down a hall of portraits of political figures partially obscured by the smoke. These strong leaders supposedly had a plan for pioneering humanity's expansion into space, saving us all from the death storm. At least those were the talking points during elections. In actuality, storm research had been an ignored priority, until now, when it was too late. I coughed again, nauseous from the nasty substance.

Myles brought me to a lobby with a desk endowed with enough laminated glass to justify a tax increase for next year. He knocked on the glass with a rat-a-tat-tat that startled a woman with a long auburn hair and a navy-blue uniform who had been absorbed by some reruns of an old show I didn't recognize.

Myles pressed a button and spoke through a speaker in the glass. "Bailey, our hero is here to save us," he said, laughing.

She turned her head slowly, almost resentfully, as if we were a minor annoyance she had been hoping she wouldn't have to deal with. Her frown confirmed this sentiment. She pressed a button on her side of the glass.

"I'm guessing the hospital isn't sending its patients," she said, nodding at my bandage.

"I was in an accident." I recalled my head injury and checked it in the reflection of the glass. It was holding up better than I thought. Bailey cupped her hand up to her ear and shrugged her shoulders.

"You have to push the button," Myles said. I nodded, and pushed the button, repeating myself.

"I see," Bailey said. "Mister…" she paused to glance at a piece of paper lying on her desk, "Fathom, is it? Wilderness First Aid Responder? Is crashing your ambulance part of some advanced emergency strategy we're not aware of?" She gave me a sideway look as if she was gauging my competency. It was a look I'd encountered a good few times over the years, and I had no redeeming retort other than to shrug my shoulders.

I shrugged my shoulders.

She let out a deflated sigh and opened a drawer producing a set of keys. "The storm's going to be full force in two hours," she said, "and it's too late to call another responder. Looks like we're trapped here for a few days."

Myles took another drag on his cigarette. "Well then, we should be head'n up to Cabell to let him know."

Bailey pulled a bulletproof glass cover over the security cameras and spent a good five minutes locking various drawers and a safe. She unlocked the door to her security station, stepped out, and locked it up again in a swift reflexive motion. She led the way across the unfurnished lobby to an elevator and unlocked a glass box containing the elevator's call button, pressing it. The elevator arrived with a loud "ding" and we stepped inside. She unlocked access to elevator controls, pressed the third-floor button, and punched in a code to allow permission of the requested action.

After an unnecessarily slow ascent, the elevator came to an abrupt halt announcing its arrival with another obnoxious "ding" and the doors opened to reveal a long hallway with high windows on either side. The windows rattled slightly as the dusty snow of the storm came up against them. Bailey walked ahead of us dangling her keys with a refined boredom. When we reached the door at the end of the hall, she unlocked it with her security card, and we stepped into a dark room emitting a dull hum of computer fans.

A man sat in front of several computer screens with his back to us. On each side of him there was a coffeemaker apparently in perpetual mid-brew—oddly excessive. Beyond his desk was a broad window with snow piled up along the edges outside.

"Ahem," Bailey announced. The man did not flinch, fixated on his work. She flicked the lights on, and he swivelled his head around with a breakneck speed.

"What the hell?" Cabell said, his face reddening as if someone had just thrown him out in the snow. He was middle-aged, perhaps mid-50s, with a buzzcut and small rectangular glasses, and he was wearing a black blazer and white shirt.

"Time for a break. You've got company."

"Eighty-five percent of the planet is consumed with an imposing cosmic matter depleting oxygen levels to eighty percent of what they used to be, and you want me to take five-minute break?"

Bailey sighed. "Would it kill you to get up and walk around once in a while?"

"Alright Bailey. Five minutes. Good advice. I'll take a break as the state of the planet slowly drops to a ten percent habitability factor, and we'll be no closer to solving the problem of this vicious storm."

"She has a point, Cabell," said Myles.

"Brief exercise will help with mental fatigue," I added.

"Who the hell is this?" Cabell asked, as he pinched the bridge of his nose.

"This our first responder. You know that type of job, right? The one that involves walking, sometimes even running and—dare I say—saving lives."

"The lives saved by officials such as myself far outweigh any in the first response or security fields. Just because you can't see the numbers in front of you doesn't make the truth of it any less real. If we don't find a solution to this imposing cosmic matter situation, we'll be heading straight into an apocalyptic scenario, and you won't be around to complain about it!"

Bailey rolled her eyes. "Well, I hate to drag you from your *exceptional work* that clearly isn't having any impact at all on the storm, but we thought you might be happy to hear that you'll be spending another few days here despite our waning food supply."

The tension of the room was interrupted by a jarring ring. Bailey pulled out her phone and looked at the screen. "I have to take this" she said, walking out of the room and leaving us wading in an awkward silence. The winds outside continued to howl, almost mocking us.

After a good minute, Cabell spoke. "So, how's that toilet coming?"

"Right. Should be unclogged in a bit. Just had a distraction, that's all," Myles said.

Bailey opened the door and gestured for us to follow her. "Roy wants us all downstairs for a videocall. You too, desk prune."

Cabell sighed, locked his computer, and made his way to the door.

We rode down the elevator and headed for the lobby, passing the familiar short hallway to the door outside. With an unexpended blast, the heavy steel door flew open blowing in wind and snow from the blizzard, offering a plump, bearded late middle-aged man dressed in a heavy fur coat, Santa cap and a backpack big enough to sustain life for months in the wilderness. We stood agape.

III

"Hi hi hi!" The man greeted us, shaking our hands, icicles dripping from his bushy, graying beard.

"Christmas's come early this year," quipped Myles, the ashes from his cigarette falling on his mop. "I didn't realize Santa Clause visited government facilities."

"Just hold it there, buddy," Bailey cautioned with her right hand, "how did you get in past the gates? Myles, did you lock the door?" Her hand dropped to her waist-high taser.

"*Ho ho ho and bottle of gin!* That's how they say it on the Bartholomew Seas, just don't be grin'n your teeth at 'em! Or, *your mother is fine company and she speaks highly of you.* No?" The man looked around the hall as if he expected some recognition for his nonsense. "Right, then, Terral B. Hylotz!"

Again, he outstretched his arm to shake hands, but we stood idle, wary of his strange behavior. He looked like he'd been homeless for years and presently his odor supported that hypothesis.

"Right. Mister...Hylotz? Interesting name. Never heard it before." Cabell paused, as if mentally perusing the many faces he'd seen in his government career. "This is a highly secured secret base, how the hell did you get in here?"

"Ah! Clever face on you. Quite square, maybe a little too pointy for my liking. Known many suits like you. No need to worry I am not here to cause trouble. You see, friends, I am from the *great outside*, in the far, far above." He spoke with the awe of a magician revealing a trick that he himself was surprised actually worked. He raised his hand in the air towards the door as if it explained everything. His tone suddenly turned reverent, his head twisted back and upwards looking at the ceiling. "It's my home, and I'll make it back there someday but for now, we will drink, we will drink!"

The cadence of his ending phrase bestowed a finality that he appeared to think would immediately bring rise to alcohol, of which there would be none. I felt bad for him. He'd ventured a bit too far into the woods. Somehow, he'd stumbled through the storms of our world's declining environmental stability to breach security at a top-secret government base. His presence created quite an enigma.

"Now just wait" Bailey scolded, waving her index finger at him, "it looks like you've a good few too many beers already. This is government property, and unless you have enough stacks in that pack of goodies to put me in early retirement, I can't let you roam around and burglarize the place.

"You can't be serious," I said. "We can't just send him off into that deadly storm, it's a miracle he survived in it at all!"

"He's trespassing on government property," Cabell insisted. "He's already broken the law. To let him go would be considerate."

"Oh, come on," I rebuked, "He's obviously confused, his pupils are dilated and he's shivering under that coat. To turn him away would be negligence!"

"Fathom's right," Myles said, "it'd be pretty damn inhumane. Wouldn't want my name pop'n up in a headline 'Janitorial Apprentice Leaves Vagrant to Die, Loses Job,

But Who Will Clean Up His Career?'"

"Enough of this," Bailey ordered, pulling out her phone. "We're obviously not going to turn him back into the storm. He can stay…for now. But we're going to need a photo for the record. Now Mr. Hylotz, please say cheese." Bailey pulled out her phone took a picture, the flash lighting up the room. Hylotz formed a wide toothy smile revealing two missing teeth and a level of carefree complacency I never thought possible. The flash reminded me of the crash. A shiver ran through my body.

"Cabell, bring everyone to the lounge. Fathom, treat him for any injuries. I'm going to print off the photo and speak with Roy. I'll be back shortly. Oh, and Myles, for God's sake, lock the damn door."

After reaching the lounge, we sat Hylotz down on a red couch next to a plant. We pulled up chairs, eager to learn more of his travels. A brown wool sweater was visible just under his winter coat.

"Now, Mr. Hylotz," Cabell asked, "exactly how have you weathered the storm out there? Studies have shown people can last no more than three hours, and that timeframe is dropping exponentially as we grow ever closer to atmospheric annihilation."

"Annihilation," Hylotz said, his arms gesturing up and down, back and forth. "Funny word. You know, if you change the sounds a bit, you can add a much better arrangement: And High Elation! That's much more friendly, wouldn't you say?" Hylotz had no grounding in reality. It was ridiculous.

"You see? Nothing but a raving lunatic," Cabell concluded.

"Lunatics? Oh yes, I've known a few of them! Wouldn't wish anyone caught in Duncan's cave. But the Ondas, now that's an ocean I'd gladly dive into."

Myles was standing idle at the door, his eyes glazed over, his cigarette nearly burned to his finger. "This guy is smoking some serious drugs," he said. "I'm completely serious—and I'm rarely serious—this guy is into some out of this world shit. And I *know* my shit. I've never seen anyone so completely and utterly fried. Maybe we should get security back here, this is completely new territory of insane."

"He's delirious," I checked his eyes with my headlight. While he'd been talking, I'd pulled out my Wilderness First Aid kit and begun the spot exam. "He is definitely suffering from hypothermia. Get him a blanket, Myles. He is acclimating to the temperature shift. He may be suffering from a head wound. Terral, can you remove your hat?"

The man removed his hat to reveal a gaping head wound. Immediately the blood made me queasy, I tried to ward off a loss of consciousness, but my head filled with stars...

...*The same moose from before appeared. How did he get into my mind?*

"Look man, sorry to interrupt your human meeting, but have you found a way to save us from this shit weather? It's a disaster out here, I mean, animal rights, and all that."

"You're an actual moose, an animal, I have no idea how you're talking to me. I don't mean to be crass but if I have a moose talking to me, I think I have more serious problems."

"Right, yet again it's so easy for humans to overlook the

suffering of animals. Look man, all I'm saying is, we could help
you out someday. We have connections, and —"

I felt the moose's voice fade into the sound of my ambu-
lance's siren. Again, the vehicle collided into a silver, metallic
object that caused an explosion of colour and stars...

"Fathom, Jesus Christ man, you OK?"

"I, uh...yeah, I'm fine." I woke up to Myles shaking
me. I felt the bandage around my head to see if I'd started
bleeding again. Thankfully I had not.

"What kind of first responder passes out at the sight of
blood?" Cabell snapped.

"Give him a break," Myles defended. "Dude's been
through a lot already. Still reeling from the accident."

"I'll be fine" I said, standing up then grabbing the bandage to treat Hylotz.

"Alright, Mr. Hylotz. You've given us quite enough of
this run-around. How about a little honesty here?" Cabell
walked up close to Hylotz and kneeled eye-to-eye with
him. "You're in trouble for even being here, at least with
some honesty you can redeem yourself and gain some
sympathy. Tell us, how did you manage to survive what
clearly has to have been at least a two month walk in the
wilderness from the city, in conditions that would see you
dead after a couple of hours?"

"Time, yes, indeed, and space; interesting concepts.
Without them, life would be meaningless. Introducing
them separates us into so many different classes, places,
'liefs—the colour of life, they say. Like the 'liefs of the
Breaus, what festive meals they have, my Breaus, I would
die to be back with my Breaus once again." Hylotz's face

grew overcast with a distinct sorrow. His type of mental disorder was hard to pinpoint. Schizophrenia, maybe, but one with a hypersensitivity to shifts between delusions.

"My friends, I think you have your answer on this fellow," Cabell sighed. Myles and I looked at each other and we knew that this man must be a crazy, rambling fool.

"Show's over," Bailey announced from the doorway, placing a photo of Hylotz she'd printed out on a side table. "I'm just off the phone with Roy, and we're going to have to lock down Hylotz in the basement. They're sending another first responder down, but it'll be a few days before they get here. Until then we are all just going to have to hamper down.

"Right. It's decided then," Cabell announced, with a satisfied resolve. There was a consensus throughout the room.

"Come on now Mr. Hylotz, we'll be taking you to a room in the basement," Bailey said. "Don't worry, it's quite homey, you'll be taken good care of. When we get back to the city, you'll get a better treatment, and maybe we'll find out where you came from."

I stood up with Hylotz and Myles and all five of us began the trek to the basement, passing the hall with the door from which Hylotz had entered. We approached the elevator to the basement.

"How's your head?" Myles asked me, grabbing the photo of Hylotz from the table

"It's fine. Only just a little woozy."

"Any more thoughts on what you hit in the accident?"

I paused. "You know, come to think of it, there was a

silver metallic object…"

"The marsh," Terral cried, and before anyone could react, he ran to the outside door and blasted back out into the storm leaving us just as bamboozled as we were when he entered.

"Well don't just stand there," Bailey ordered, "We can't have him running around the base. We've got to stop him!"

IV

"Terral B. Hylotz." Bailey's words echoed through the lobby as she tucked her auburn hair into the fluffy hood of her blue winter coat. "What an unusual name."

"Not from the east, that's for sure," I said. "Homeless, maybe, from the south side?"

"He smelled like marijuana and regret," Cabell said, wrapping a blue scarf around his neck, while grabbing a walnut brown winter coat from the closet in the hall.

"Don't judge a book by it's cover. He could be a genius for all you know." Myles pulled on a white winter jacket.

Bailey opened the door to a security closet and removed a couple of two-way radios from an old emergency kit that had ceased production over a decade ago. "Hylotz may need on-the-spot medical attention, are you OK to come along Fathom?"

"I'm fine," I said, pulling a white cap over my head.

"I just don't get how he could have got past the security walls of the perimeter," Cabell said. "They're over sixty feet high and they completely block off the area. He'd have to have come by water or air and both are near completely impossible with the storm."

"All the more reason for us to stop him," Bailey said.

"Who knows who else he's with, or what he's capable of. His confused appearance could be a front or a distraction for some other effort. Now listen, the radio's set on channel one. Fathom and I will take one each. Stick together and don't spend more than an hour max out in the storm. No matter what, come back after an hour." Bailey took a box of face shields from the closet and passed us each one. We pulled them on. "Ready?"

"Don't forget this," Myles said, tossing something that careened through the air before gliding to a landing on the floor in front of Bailey. She picked up the photo of Hylotz that Myles had folded into a paper airplane. She sighed, tucking the photo in her coat pocket.

We looked around the room at each other. With mismatched winter coats, face shields, snow-boots, furry mittens and caps, we looked more like Christmas carollers than a search team. And we certainly had nothing to sing about.

"Let's go!" Bailey said, pushing open the heavy iron door to the storm outside.

We trudged down the wheelchair ramp with boots squishing the snow. For the most part, we were like clunky, unarmed soldiers. Bailey locked the base twirling the key around her finger. The storm had settled somewhat. Gentle cyclones lifted snowflakes into the air, dropping them off wherever they might disappear in a gust of wind.

A treeline became visible through the blurry white, with a dip where the bridge to the road was. Behind us, the base stretched high up into the night air, its searchlight strobing through the cold mess of snow. Once it would have guided ships to shore, now it remained a last-resort cosmic beacon begging for divine intervention to come save us from the storm.

"Got him!" Myles yelled, slightly left of path.

"What?" Bailey asked.

"Got his footprints!"

We walked over find him staring at a path of bulky footprints. They trailed off towards the bridge.

"Good job," Bailey said.

We followed the footprints to the bridge. A glimpse of the sea below reminded me that a small misstep could be fatal. At the end of the bridge, we stood idle, scanning the snow for the footprint trail.

We continued, heading in the direction the footprints had been going. We passed a vacant parking lot, then made it to the road. It was dark. Bailey pulled out flashlights for us each from her backpack, when a gust of wind roared through the air. The photo airplane she had placed in her pocket became airborne, and she fell back into the snow. She pulled herself back up and shook snow off her coat. We continued, heading towards the woods.

"I've got something," Cabell shouted. There was another trail of footprints, but it was drifting into the woods. We peered through the snowclad trees, hesitant, but we knew Bailey had no intention of stopping.

As we headed into the woods, the ankle-length snow was hindering, but manageable. The wind was freezing though. Disorienting. The light from our flashlights led us through the shadows with Hylotz meandering footprints becoming harder and harder to spot. We passed a small pond frozen over with ice.

"Oh no," Cabell said, looking off to the side.

"What is it?" Myles asked.

Cabell held up a boot which was, to our dismay, quite likely the property of Hylotz. "There is a small hole in the ice."

I shook my head. "It doesn't bode well for him if he is walking around without a boot. He'll need medical attention. We need to find him fast."

"That could be a problem," Cabell said. "Look." He pointed at the footprints we'd been following, which were now accompanied by two or three more smaller ones, hoofprints? Hylotz's footprints became indistinguishable. They forked into two different paths: one up, one down.

"We're going to have to split up," said Bailey. "Cabell, you join me. Myles and Fathom, you can take the left path."

"Right. Fair enough, lets go Fathom," Myles said.

We branched off from the other two and walked up the path. As it became darker, the cliff jutted out impeding our progress, and eventually we had no choice but to scale the cliff. Myles stopped, refusing to proceed. "I... can't," he said.

"You can't climb?"

"No I mean, I can but..." Myles paused, as if searching for the right words to use. "Look, I did a lot of wilderness expeditions as a kid. "There's something about being out here that just...brings back some bad feelings. I really need a smoke, maybe I should head back..."

"We can't head back! We've got to find Hylotz. Look,

I made it to the base on foot and I can tell you, it's not the kind of situation you want to be alone in. It's very disorienting, and you can lose your way. If we split up that leaves one of us without a radio. It's not a good scenario. It's really not that steep and there's no other way forward. If it gets much steeper, we'll turn back, OK?"

Myles paused, deep in thought. "Alright," he said. "Let's go."

It didn't take too long before we reached the top of the cliff. The storm had eased off, allowing us a limited view of the snowy forest below. The now-faintly-visible footprints led us to the subtle moonlit glow of a clearing. I paused. Something felt off.

"What are you waiting for?" Myles asked.

Then I saw it. Nearly perfectly camouflaged against a cliff wall, there was an outline of something…some, creature. I felt an immediate spike of adrenaline, a heightening of my senses and tingling my skin with goosebumps.

"…There…" I said, nodding my head in the direction of the figure. Myles turned and pointed his flashlight directly at a moose looming with intimidating antlers staring straight at us. The moose did not move. Suddenly, I recalled the crash in my mind. *Did I hit a moose?* Something felt wrong about it all.

"Relax," Myles said. "It won't hurt us. It's not angry."

"Damn right I'm not angry."

I shivered as the realization hit me. Somehow, I could understand what the moose was thinking.

"Fathom man, you ok?"

"Look man, no qualms with you," the moose said. *"You can help us."*

"Myles, I think…I…need to sit down."

"Relax, the moose won't hurt us. We can just back up and leave…"

"He's right. Not going to hurt you. But you need to help us. All of us. Otherwise, things are gonna get messy."

My mind blanked. I knew, somehow, this moose could understand my thoughts.

"What do you want from me?" I thought, towards the moose.

"Man, we don't have the answers right now. But there are others, far away, there are many of us, and there is suffering. We need your help to stop it. We know you can hear us and we know the humans have tricks against the storm they are only now coming to learn. But with your help we can all benefit together, instead of fighting against each other to survive."

"Fathom man, come on, lets go!"

"What do you want from us?" I asked.

"We don't know everything right now. But we do know that you have been looking for the bearded old man, and we know of his travels. Many of us have spent time with him as well, and he holds the key to all of our struggles. And we know which way he went."

The moose moved aside to reveal a dark hole in the cliffside. It walked back into the woods. Myles shone his light towards the cliff. "A cave?"

He shone his light inside to reveal the outline of a person huddled over to conserve heat.

"Fathom, hand over the two-way!" I passed it to him. "Come in! Bailey, Cabell, Come in!"

"We have you. What is it?" Cabell's voice beamed through the radio.

"We got him."

V

The cave was eerily quiet compared to the storm outside. Myles approached with slow footsteps, but as he neared, it became evident that this was not a person, but instead a backpack.

"Well now," Myles said, picking up the backpack and looking inside. "What gifts did he leave for us? We've got some bags of leaves, a pipe and a lighter. Definitely smoker materials, but I've never seen these types of plants before." Myles shone the light further into the cave. Hylotz was nowhere to be seen. Another snowy entrance was vaguely visible at the end. I began heading towards the exit, only to turn to find Myles fiddling with the lighter.

"Myles!" I said. "This is no time to smoke, we've got to rendezvous with the others."

Myles put the lighter back in the backpack and lifted it over his shoulders, and we left through the second exit. There was a thick patch of bushes and a short decline down a hill, and we were back on the asphalt of the road to the base, not too far from the locked gate leading back to the city.

It was clear and quiet, like we were in the eye of the storm. Over the cliff, the ocean stretched on, clouded with splotches of the white storm like voluminous plumes of smoke flowing from an inextinguishable fire up into space. Flashlights flickered in the distance. It was Bailey and Cabell.

While we waited for them to catch up, I realized we were standing exactly where my ambulance had gone off the road. I could see the tire marks heading into the woods. Another path veered off to our left, into a small clearing.

"What is it?" Bailey asked.

"Wait," I said and walked towards the path of the object that had hit me. I motioned for her and the others to follow.

We entered the clearing. A big shiny triangular object sparkled through the trees. Rays of moonlight hit the metallic silver, creating a surreal sparkling. I'd seen nothing like it before.

"Not sure you should go near that" Cabell said. I ignored him, reaching out to feel the surface. It was oddly warm.

"Wow," Myles said, piecing it together. "*This* hit you?"

"Yes," I said. It was all making sense now. I replayed the crash in my mind.

"Well, you should probably step away—" the object flashed forcing me to jump back. The smooth metallic outer surface had disappeared in four spaces on either side of the structure, offering a clear view right through its dark interior. With padded seating, it certainly looked like a vehicle, but there was no apparent apparatus other than a black steering wheel.

"Careful," Bailey said.

I took another step back. "What's that down by the door?" I said, pointing at a colorful item lodged between the object and snow. Bailey picked it up out of the snow to reveal the photo airplane.

"What are the chances of that?" Bailey said, laughing. She walked around the object touching it gently, just like I had done. Then she sat inside.

Myles unloaded the backpack into the object and jumped in as well. "Come on Cabell," he said.

"Not my cup of tea at all," Cabell said. "I really need to get back to the washroom, can we please just head back to the base?"

"It's much warmer in here," I said, holding my hand in against the soft material of the seat. And it was. You could feel the heat emanating from inside, yet there was no heating device visible. There was enough space for about four people.

"Come on, Cabell. This is *some* device." Bailey began running her hands along what was apparently a dashboard, and the slippery surface seemed to bend, receptive to her hand.

Cabell, shivering, stepped inside.

"What could it be?" Myles said. "Very strange."

"It's not government technology" Cabell said. "Being an authority, I can say that—unless it's classified, but we stopped experimenting with classified vehicles after the arrival of the death storm."

"Well come on Fathom," Bailey said. "Jump in."

Who will take the pilot's seat?

Fathom   **Bailey**
Continue Reading   Go to Page 43

FATHOM PILOTS

I jumped through door. My seat was calmingly smooth and lukewarm. There was a flash of light from the dashboard, and the panel came to life with bizarre neon green symbols as wiry tentacles lashed out grasping my arms. The interior glowed bright green from the dashboard. The others shouted, banging against the closed doors.

The thing jolted to life. Unburdened by any apparent propulsion system, it simply rose with the cyclones of the storm. It accelerated at a suicidal pace, and through the windows, we could see the clouds of the storm over the water becoming more frequent, until our view was obfuscated by a white blur of snow.

We began to spin. The ship turned faster and faster, and it was getting colder, colder, freezing! The screaming, the spinning, it all coalesced into a piercing high pitch tone in my mind, and I felt as if I was falling apart stretching into a bitter… cold… *space*…

I trembled. My anxiety peaked. The stormy whiteness prevailed. I felt tiny, like I'd been compacted into a snowflake. Doorways appeared on my left and right, scrolling past me. I was fly-

ing through a long, drab hospital hall. Patients were belligerent, yelling at hospital staff. It felt like the worst encounters of my entire career all infused together. A window appeared at the end of the hall. Before I could consider the fact that I would really prefer not to crash through the damn thing, I crashed through the damn thing.

Still white, but now, control. The snow was mushy in my fingers. I pushed myself upward. Snowclad trees were all around. They were like the ones near the Last Bastion base, but the snowfall was lighter here. It was a pleasant departure from harsher conditions I was used to facing. The flashing red and blue lights of emergency vehicles appeared through the trees.

I approached a highway just like the one near Last Bastion. The ambulances and police cars were lit, but empty. A single gurney stood alone in the middle of the vehicles. I had no desire to be here, even though this was my entire occupation. I approached the gurney. A sheet was pulled over a body. There was no movement. Were they dead?

Through the corner of my eye, I caught an outline along the treeline of figures, no, creatures. Gigantic antlers. Moose. Many, many moose. They were moving just slightly, their dark silhouettes only vaguely discernable against the darkness of the receding forest.

I suppressed the desire to run, but my heart was racing wild. Where could I go, anyway? I had no idea where the hell I was. With great trepidation, I reached my hand to the sheet covering the body and pulled it back slowly.

The figure sat up immediately, his bloody old face shocked me, his toothless grin shot me staggering back several steps. Blood soaked through his graying beard. I felt the urge to pass out, to run away, to leave this horrible job forever. But some-

how, I couldn't.

The old man winked at me and pulled out a big brown pipe, lighting it. A few of the moose from the trees walked out. As the man smoked then exhaled, a feeling of ease washed over me. The apprehension and tension of the situation abated into a serene acceptance.

The man shuffled off the gurney and joined the moose as they walked back into the woods. I stared as they disappeared, at a complete loss as to what to say or think.

The winds quickly snowballed into a roar as the brutality of the blizzard returned. Again, I became immersed in white, and my vision began to quake as if shaking out of existence.

Was that Hylotz?

COMA CLUSTER
WITH: FATHOM

I woke to radiant sunlight glowing through the glass of the ship. The rays heated the air inside that surrounded my hunched body as if I were wrapped in the womb. The others were asleep.

Through the front window, I absorbed the breathtaking view. A vibrant valley with a lush evergreen forest extending off into mountains with snow-capped peaks. A bustling river wove into a lake near the horizon. The sunlight cast an iridescent brilliance speckling the sky with a rainbow of sorts: the entire spectrum of visible light was stretched on display like the palette of some epistemological artist. It seemed too beautiful to be real.

I opened the pilot door and a greater warmth immediately struck me, a stark contrast to our former predicament. Moreover, I was moved by the sounds outside. The chirps, the tweets, and the new sounds that I'd never heard before. There was a sense of an overwhelming presence of abundance; new, curious, evolving life.

I walked out into the rushing water and knelt down to feel it. It was tepid and smooth, unlike the freezing cold water near the Last Bastion base. It was perfect. Where the hell were we?

Rising to my feet again, I walked to the edge of the river, sending grasshoppers dashing left and right in reaction to me. Squirrels paused along the treeline, as if in contemplation of my arrival. As I began walking again, some of them dashed up into their trees, that were reminiscent of the Grand Firs of the island I grew up on.

I made my way down the river with a fascinated curiosity. I came upon a couple of deer enjoying a drink of water along the river. As I approached, they looked up, and I was immediately filled with a thought of *who the hell is that guy?*

That was weird.

Nevertheless, I continued on making my way into the forest. The soundscape was filled with insects whizzing past, water rustling, grasshoppers chirping and birds singing. The gentle wind brushed against my skin.

I entered a small clearing with two rabbits in the distance. I stood to watch them for a moment, absorbing my surroundings and I realized I could hear their thoughts.

"Jack from Paradama lost another two bunnies. Hunters ramping up 'cuz of the storm."

"Shocking."

"Waste, really. Holds no candle to the wrath of the Bies, though. Thousands of humans killed as a result of them."

"I'd like to say it's their own fault."

"Oh, definitely is, they don't deserve it though."

"No, no."

"Shame we can't reach either of them. I heard that…"

A stick cracked under my foot. When I looked back up, the rabbits were scampering away. Christ. What the hell was this? It all seemed so surreal, yet, at the same time, it was very clearly happening.

Making my way further through the forest, I heard a crying in the distance. I worked towards the sound to find a placid clearing with a waterfall. The source of the sound was a deer calf caught in a foothold trap, crying and unable to escape. I cautiously made my way to it. The poor creature sprung away from me as I approached, tearing its ankle with each attempt.

My heart raced and I felt an obligation to help immediately, but at the same time I felt a strong hesitation pulling me back to the ship. I reached down and pushed on the levers allowing the jaws of the trap to open. The deer scampered away.

The sunlight faded quickly, as if dialed back, casting the forest into an ominous late evening darkness. When I turned around, the treeline was peppered with a sea of eyes staring at me. Their stillness was petrifying, at first, causing my heart to race again. Then, as before with the rabbits, their thoughts flooded over me like a tidal wave.

"Is this him?"

"He looks awfully pudgy; does he eat deer?"

"Quite a puzzling thought, he is, for sure."

"Should we bring him to Aarth?"

My heartbeat slowed, as I realized they meant no harm. They began to depart slowly, all walking together back through the woods, and I felt myself drawn to them with a childlike curiosity. We spent a good half hour traversing up a steep incline before reaching a mountain peak with an amazing view of the forest below. It stretched on to the setting sun on the horizon.

Finally, we reached an adjacent mountain peak with bushes packed together like a giant couch, and a single moose stretched out, leisurely surveying the area while, somehow, smoking a joint.

"Ah, the helper. Good to see you man," the moose was so casual in its speech, as if it had been waiting for me. It tapped the joint against a rock and took another inhale. I am not sure how this was possible, the logistics of it were beyond me.

"Hi?" I thought, stupefied. With my mouth agape and my brow dipping, I'm sure I appeared like a deer in head-lights.

"Yes, hello, and all those foolish human formalities. I can imagine you're confused about the whole thing, understandable. We've been watching you for a bit now. You're the second human we've found to be 'sensitive' to our language."

I continued to stare at the moose, perplexed.

"Look man, truth is, the track record for humans and, er, what do you call us? Moose? It hasn't been the greatest, and it's gotten even worse during the storm. We need someone to step up and take the reins for us, to use a very human analogy.

"We've been able to read humans for a while, and there's unfortunately not much to like. Humans have subjected Moose and other animals to some pretty dire conditions, sticking us in cages, running us over with vehicles, feeding some us some god-awful gruel stuff, which to be honest, is absolutely disgusting food that—highly unrecommended. I must say, you name it, humans have done it, and that all really has to stop.

"With the storm happening, human behavior has only got-ten worse. Humans are killing us left, right, and center in a mad panic to survive the storm.

"*We're not sure how you've been able to understand us, nor how you've managed to visit us in our ethereal home, but this violence has to stop. We're all working together to beat this storm, and it's time you joined our pacifist fight instead of being an enemy in it.*"

"*Uhm. How exactly can I do that?*" I asked.

"*Ah, yes, my dude. As you're beginning to figure out by now, but this whole construct you've spent the last hour in has been our best effort to communicate with you. It's not real. It's our best mutual exclamation of peace between our worlds.*"

I paused. It wasn't real. This made sense. It was all some sort of illusion. So, if that was the case, where the hell was I?"

"*You say you want me to help,*" I said, "*but I have no idea where the hell I am or what I possibly could do to help. Being a spokesman for an entire species isn't in the job description, especially not in the midst of an apocalypse. I'm just a medical responder, and not that good a one to boot. Given the events of the past few hours I'm quite ready to quit this whole first responding business.*

The moose pulled his joint out of his snout, and exhaled a puff of smoke in my face, sending me into a coughing fit. "*Woah there, man, settle down. I've never seen anyone so high-strung. You're our best hope right now. Buck up, have some faith in yourself. Anyway, look, there's a world far from here—Kostroma—where a group of our species—The Bies—has gone wild in retribution against humans. We don't know how exactly you can do it, but if you can get there, you can help stop them by trying to reach a truce between them and humans. Just reason with them. We've tried, but they've become exceedingly aggressive since the storm, mirroring the humans that once lived there."*

The moose again inhaled smoke through its lungs, and exhaled, causing the puff to swirl around its head, reminding me of the storm. As I stood there considering the situation, I felt the whole landscape shaking. I reached out to the moose for help, but everything went black.

◢

"Fathom! Fathom!"

My body shook with a brutal force. I felt myself shake from a sleepiness to come face-to-face with Bailey.

"Hey, he's not dead!" she said. "How comforting."

"What...happened?"

"You were out for a good hour!"

"I..." My speech drifted off as I stared out at a massive colourful nebula in front of us which was interspersed with the white snowy powder of the storm.

"Goddamn ship took 'us right up into space!" Myles said from the back seat.

"Yes, and we'd really like to try to get back to earth *right now*," Cabell said.

"Move aside, first responder, I'm going to bring us home." Bailey pulled me into her seat and took the wheel.

BAILEY PILOTS

As Bailey took the pilot's seat, wiry tentacles jumped out and wrapped around her skin. The ship jumped head-first into the storm. The entire interior glowed a bright green as the ship rotated in circles. The view through the windshield was blocked by the intense white of the storm. And then all grasp on reality seemed to acquiesce to that of another…

The frosty white of the storm dispersed, revealing a bright azure sky with a beautiful orange-red sun settling along the dusky beige of the rocky Nevada mountain range. With a blurry haze, it was an incredibly realistic memory of my military deployment when the world first encountered the storm. The nostalgia was bittersweet. In these last days, the world was incredibly naïve to the severity of the storm.

"Ten bucks says you hit the cactus Bailey," Jim laughed. To my left, his bronzy calloused face beamed with a silly grin as he passed me the bow. Ah, archery. It was the one escape that we all loved.

Publicly, we were deployed to monitor for UFOs due to increased sightings as the storm grew more prevalent. But we were really tracking the Storm Ninjas: a cult of UFO conspiracy theorists that believed the universe was run by alien lizards disguised as politicians. At first they were harmless, carrying out ridiculous attempts at storming Area 51. But over time, they'd obtained some serious black-market weaponry, and had carried out some moderately successful attacks.

"Ten bucks is nothing," I snickered. "Fifty bucks. Bullseye."

Jim and the others laughed knowing full well no money would change hands. I took the bow and grabbed an arrow. I pulled it back against the string as I lined up my shot. Before I could shoot, an arrow whizzed past my head.

I blinked twice. Someone else had taken a shot. The arrow was lodged in the centre of the board. I turned my head to see a man placing his bow on our table, his back to us. It was our Major, Richardson. I instantly remembered his shape in the camo uniform. With decades of experience, his skill as a soldier was far superior to ours. He had a passion for the field and an unending ambition that had become non-existent nowadays.

As he faced us, it quickly became apparent that this was not Richardson, but a man with a graying beard and a toothless smile. I lowered my bow, trying to recall where I'd seen his face before. But the colours began to fade as the dusty storm closed in once again. The white cold surrounded me.

Could that have been Hylotz?

PART TWO
ATAVIKA
WITH: BAILEY

I

The bitter cold pulsed through my body. The ship's steering wheel shook in my grip. The storm obstructing the windshield disappeared in brief moments, offering glimpses of a giant sun on the horizon. The others screamed as we continued to jolt violently back and forth in our seats.

Clearly this was my version of hell. I'd detested mandatory flight training so strongly it had nearly turned me off the military completely. My first experience in a virtual flight machine drove me to vomit on my co-pilot, bestowing me with the nickname 'Palely Bailey.' That familiar nausea returned.

The storm receded as we entered a clearing with misty clouds scattered below like a rink in a stadium open to the vastness of space above. This momentary serenity fleeted as the ship dropped into the clouds below, skimming along like a stone on the ocean. Try as I might, I could not regain control. Through the motion blur of clouds, quick brushes of green appeared peaking through the white like blotches on a canvas. Trees. But hardly the 'happy little trees' of Bob Ross; these trees were monstrous, daunting.

With the volatility of the ship, we'd be on a crash course if I didn't act fast. I put all my force against the wheel to push it up. As if mocking my incompetence, the ship took a nosedive into the sea of clouds below. Before I could realize my error and correct it, we abruptly hit a tree, and the ship spun and convulsed as we hit another tree and all control was lost. The ship hopelessly tore through branches. I shivered, realizing I may just have sealed our fate.

My head was spinning. A static of rain persisted from outside. Glossy verdant leaves drooped over the windshield. I reached for the door and the ship teetered at my movement. The others stirred.

"Be careful," Fathom said. "We're barely stable."

The ship eased back as I pulled my arm away from the door handle. Again, I remembered my first training missions, where the door to the VR machine was like a lifeline. That sense of security was stripped from me now.

"What's out there?" Myles asked, trying to get a look through the windshield. The view was severely obstructed by the tangled leaves, but a maze of vines stretched beyond into the distance.

A jungle. Somehow, we'd landed right in the middle of a goddamn jungle.

"It's incredible," Cabell said, "how this ship has transported us so fast. This technology is mesmerizing."

"I'd be happy to have never found it," I said. Again, I felt a magnetic pull towards the ship's door, like the reflexive impulse to lock up Last Bastion. My conditioned instincts emboldened by years in security were useless

here. "We can't just sit here. We've got to do something."
Again, I reached for the handle.

"Bailey, no," Myles said, but it was too late. As I
reached, the ship tipped with my weight. I was careful,
but it had now gained a momentum of its own.

"Oh my God," Fathom said.

"Jump out," Cabell yelled, and we all grabbed for the
door handles causing the ship to lose its balance, falling
off whatever was holding it up.

I jumped out through door's opening and soared
through the air. One of the vines I'd seen earlier came
into view and I desperately reached for it, barely holding
on. The screams of the others faded into echoes below as
my freefall momentum came to an abrupt smack against
some surface.

➤

A sweltering heat much heavier than a sauna struck
me with unrelenting ferocity. The only salvation was the
constant showering of raindrops soaking through my
clothes. Slowly, I pushed myself to a sitting position and
removed my jacket out of a pure primal desire to reduce
the heat.

Beyond the insulating sound of rain there was a dull
chorus of cicadas occasionally interrupted by the chirping of birds and the occasional grunts of monkeys. I shivered from chaos of it all. What other animals could be out
there?

The glowing light of the sun loomed high overhead,
beaming through a bushy canopy revealing a daunting
maze of jungle trees before me. The trees themselves had
trunks thicker than skyscrapers and were laden with tan-

gly vines. The surface below me felt rough and bumpy; a rugged dark bark of a tree branch that extended down far below. I crawled to my left to try to look over the edge, but no jungle bottom was visible. The view extended into darkness. The view upwards was equally indeterminable, and the storm was vaguely visible through the trees in the distance.

My memory was drawn to the war movies I'd seen as a child and revisited many times throughout my life: Arizona Blood and Hurting, but also classic remakes like Apocalypse Now, Rambo and Jurassic Park…there were so many that reflected the dark, ominous scene before me. A rumbling of thunder in the distance disrupted these memories.

"The first rule of operating a spaceship is don't open the door," said Cabell, his voice seemingly appearing from nowhere.

"Christ," I said, jumping back. I looked up to see him standing above me. "How about 'the first rule of crashing in a jungle is don't sneak up on the pilot,'" I said with a frown.

"I'm sorry, but you have really landed us in a situation here. Myles and Fathom are nowhere to be seen. It looks like they may have fallen to their death."

I shuddered. Was it so? Had my action led to their deaths? It must be so. The drop was deadly. I needed to process this.

"Our major rainforests were irreparably damaged during at the start of our current phase of the death storm, but this one is unscathed. It looks like you've taken us *very far* from—"

"Just hold on," I said, raising to my feet, "You know damn well that ship is a wildcard, there's no controlling it. Fathom drove us up into space. I could barely land the thing, and—"

"Of course, I know that," Cabell said, his glasses blurry and wet from the rain. He was awkwardly holding a giant leaf over his head which had very little shielding effect. The poor fool was raised with a silver spoon. He was the type who couldn't operate an umbrella and would just give up and throw it away when he couldn't close it. "Look, lets just focus on getting out of here and back home, OK? We need to find the ship so I can get back to my office."

"You you *you*, everything is about *you*." I frowned at him. He had never faced a real struggle in his life. No appreciation for the common man, endlessly protected by the naïve leisure of his ivory tower.

"What the hell is your problem with me?"

I shot him a resentful glance. "Must be your glasses. Have you tried corrective surgery?" He shook his head.

"Look, we've got to work together if we're going to get out of here. When I jumped out of the ship, I landed on this branch, and the ship continued falling through the branches below. It has got to be down there somewhere. So let's start working our way down."

Ahead of us, the branch met a steep decline which was unpassable. We chose to follow the branch behind us, which extended off into the distance. We began our apprehensive descent downward.

We passed over curious platforms formed of wood planks. Clearly, there was civilized life here. It was a relief.

"Lets just hope they're friendly," Cabell said.

As we headed downward, the surrounding sounds grew louder, and we were occasionally bothered by eyes watching us from dense bushes growing on the branches.

Our spirits raised again, when we reached a vine bridge that joined two branches. The bridge itself was small, with the same wood used for the platforms. Vines roped it together. It was dangerous but passable. We cautiously edged along it.

"It can barely support our weight," said Cabell. "How small can the folks who created it be?"

A branch snapped behind us. We spun around. Nothing.

"Who's there?" I demanded. Still nothing. I shivered. We continued.

"The consistency of the wooden plateaus and the bridges indicate some form of civilization," said Cabell, "however their level of intelligence—we can't be sure."

Another snap. We spun around on our bridge. Again, nothing. I reached down for my trusty taser. Still there, thank God.

The rain was a serious impediment to our progress, and we quickly tired of it. The stress of the past few hours was finally catching up and I realized that I needed rest.

"Where can we stop?" I said, as we hit another plateau. Cabell turned and looked at me, then scanned the area.

"Well, I don't know. We'll have to keep going until

we find something. If there is something following us, I mean—let's just keep looking."

I nodded.

We continued for another good twenty minutes or so. I felt like I'd pass out at any moment.

"Here, look at this," Cabell said, "there's some crack in the trunk here but it's…it doesn't look natural. It looks forced open. The edges here are carved as if…cut by a blade."

We edged inside through a narrow opening. My claustrophobia started up, but as soon as I hit the floor on the inside, it was quickly suppressed by my desire to sleep. I began to address Cabell and I think he said something, but any recollection of a conversation quickly faded as I fell into a deep, highly anticipated, sleep.

"They're in the mountains!" Jim's voice crackled over the chilly mist of the enclosing storm as we followed in hot pursuit of the Storm Ninjas. Capturing them in their desert base was exacerbated by the storm, but we had finally cornered them.

Gunfire echoed across the mountains. I shuddered at the memory. Richardson ordered us to withdraw and regroup temporarily to come up with a better plan.

"We need to get out now," I'd insisted.

"We've never had a better chance to get them than now," Richardson said. We knew there was no going against his decision. He would never have ordered the attack if he didn't have to. I hated that he'd been forced to put us all in harm's way.

We took an offensive approach from left of the base, but somehow, they'd known. To this day I don't know how they could have known. They attacked us with assault rifles in an amateur-

ism so irrational, it could have only worked in the hands of the insane.

We were forced to draw back, but not before Richardson took heat. His cry still tears through my nightmares. I'd tried to go back but the gunfire was too intense. We were forced to retreat and make it back home in the deadly storm which had rendered our navigational instruments useless. Richardson became one of the first deaths by cause of storm exposure.

A loud roar reverberated through my bones. It shook me awake. The air was hot and humid. I put my hand out to feel the dry, rough texture of the tree. I remembered the jungle. Christ. How was it possible to wake up to a worse reality than Nevada?

I reached for Cabell, but he was not nearby. I found his glasses on the floor, only to be shaken by another terrifying roar, much closer.

II

I waited. There were no sounds outside. I carefully edged my way out through the hole, cautiously peeking out.

There was no rain. A noxious smoke filled the air. It was rising from down below. This was worse than the Last Bastion base. I coughed. A small figure about a yard away disappeared into a bush.

"Hey," I yelled. No response. They were too short to be Cabell. I walked out and looked around. Nothing. I walked towards the bush. The figure jumped out and ran down along the tree branch. They were dressed head-to-toe in leaves.

"Hey," I shouted, "I just want to talk."

A tiger-like creature jumped from a bush nearby. It roared. In a split second I ran, and the creature chased me, lashing out at my leg. I tripped and fell but picked myself up. The creature was positioning to pounce on me. I screamed and desperately dove over the edge of the tree branch.

I fell three or four branches down before catching a vine of one of the bridges, but it immediately snapped. The bridge fell and I fell with it. I came up hard against a tree trunk with just enough power in my legs to keep me from suffering the brunt of the force.

I struggled to climb the vine. Decades ago, I would have had no trouble. Still, I managed to pull myself up onto the branch, where I lay back with my eyes closed, panting. When I opened my eyes, there were two more staring back at me. I sat up quickly. A short, scraggly brown-haired woman stared at me. Her face was sooty from smoke. She was wearing an outfit composed of leaves.

"Hello," I said.

We stared at each other uneventfully for a good two minutes. Could she speak English?

"Hello," she replied. The silence seemed to go on forever. I had many questions snowballing inside me.

"What is your name?" I asked.

"Maya," she replied.

"I am Bailey," I said, unsure how she would respond to a handshake and realizing that formality would probably be lost on her. "Are there others like you?"

"We are the Uriah," she said, nodding her head. I coughed at the smoke.

"This is quite a transportation system you have set up," I nodded towards a nearby vine bridge. "But where is all this smoke from?"

"The Uri. They praise the gods of the forest." I nodded, unsure of the reasoning behind this custom.

"Maya, did you see a man with me?"

"There was a man. Yes. But when I came back, he was gone."

I coughed again. "Where can we get away from this smoke?" I asked.

"Follow me."

I followed her down the tree branch. We crossed more bridges. I had to cover my mouth at times to avoid coughing from the smoke. We carefully scaled vines secured down along a trunk. We made it to another trunk with water flowing over it from high above. Maya walked into the water and disappeared. I carefully followed. The tree had been hollowed out into an area with jugs crafted from wood that contained water. Light shinned in from slits carved in bark.

Maya passed me a jug and I drank much of the water in it. She passed a coconut cut into pieces. It was the first food I'd had in hours. She explained that she was a water-carrier for the Uriah, who lived high above in the jungle worshipping the sun. The Uri lived far below and were hated by the Uriah, who forbid any communication with outsiders. She had met a few Uri and smoked with them and wished to visit the great ocean below.

After our discussions Maya said that she had to bring water to the Uriah village above. I decided to stay in this small home, partially because I needed rest, and partially because I was afraid the Uriah would not accept me. When she left, I lay down and drifted into another sleep.

"So all you have to do is stare at monitors all night?" The young man grinned at me with his arms back, his fingers interlocked behind his head and his feet on the desk.

"Put your feet down," I said. "But yes, that's it. Just stick to the routine patrols and you'll be fine. No napping."

"This is a cinch."

"It's a good job, but you could be a little more respectful." He just stared at me, expression blank and naïve. I sighed. The kid's mother owned a security business downtown. Nepotism was rampant these days. Most businesses had closed, and it was unsafe to be outside for more than a day. Security positions were dying out, but big corporations still needed protection from the growing hoards of homeless people breaking into commercial spaces seeking refuge from the storm.

"Any reason why that barrel is on fire?" The kid asked. I glanced at an amber glow on one of the monitors. The alley at the back of the factory was vacant, but the fire was growing bigger.

"Looks like we've got some excitement. Got your taser? Good. This'll be a good exercise for your first day." I flicked on my radio. "We're investigating a fire in the back alley, will advise of outcome."

I locked up the security cabinet and grabbed the fire extinguisher, passing it to the kid. "Know how to operate one of these?" He rolled his eyes at me.

We stepped out of the security room and locked the doors, beginning the ten-minute walk down the hall towards the back of the factory.

The alleys were a target for loitering as they offered a little better protection from the storm. Although shelters were set in place for the homeless, they were overburdened and lacking in rations. Often, people would brave the storm to dumpster-dive for more food. It was becoming riskier, though, as the storm grew more volatile.

When we reached the door, I unlocked and pushed the door open in a single swoop. "Hello? Anyone out here?"

The cold night air was crisp with the type of chill that would quickly freeze your face. The snow between buildings was gentle, less stirred than in the streets, where it gained more momentum with the wind. The alley was vacant except for a dumpster near the corner, which led to another alley leading to the street.

The fire was not too far from the door. I nodded at the kid, who walked over and sprayed the fire, and I had to admit, I was surprised he knew how to operate the damn thing. Smoke from the extinguished fire rose along the buildings, disappearing in the pale white of the storm.

Something soared through the air and landed next to the kid, and he had to shuffle to the side to avoid it. A person in a hoodie emerged from behind the dumpster and ran out of the alley.

"Hey," I shouted, my heart pumping from the attack. It was rare these days to catch someone in the alley, and interactions were usually more amicable. Weapons were unlikely, but the possibility was always in the back of my mind.

I walked over to the kid. He was picking up the tossed item. He passed it to me.

A snow globe.

Ornaments like this had been a cash grab in the early days of the storm, where there was excitement for the new lockdown *style of living. Within the globe, snow swirled around a small candle-lit cottage, nestled in a forest, protected by thick glass.*

I shook my head and tossed the globe in the dumpster. "Come on kid, we've got another patrol."

Voices interrupted my dream. They were speaking in a language I didn't understand. It was dark. Night? Blurry lights glowed through the waterfall. They were getting closer. I fought back the urge to go outside.

A torch was passed around the waterfall and placed inside, then a small figure about the size of Maya jumped through the water, their face masked by a skull. The teeth were crooked, and the eyes were cut out. I screamed.

Another two figures in skull masks joined and ran to me, I fought them, but they knocked me over the head.

I woke, still dizzy from the knock. I had no idea how much time had passed. Light bounced around the room casting eerie shadows against the wall. In the middle, a fire had been set, and the skull masked figures stood around it. Cabell, Myles, Fathom and Maya were all strapped up against the wall and Fathom and Myles were struggling to break free. Thank God they were still alive. I pulled my arms forward realizing I had been bound. The voices of the skull group chanted in some unintelligible language.

"What are they saying?" I shouted at Maya.

"They say, 'we hate foreigners,'" Maya replied. "'Foreigners fill the air with poison. They burn the forest. They must die by their fire. The god of light will save us from the poison fools.'"

The skull group moved towards us with torches in their hands.

"They can't be serious," I shouted. "What have we ever done to them?"

"We don't have anything to do with setting the forest on fire!" Cabell shouted, but they ignored him. The others shouted and screamed to no avail. My chest tightened and my heart jumped into overdrive as the skull figure approached. I twisted my head in a vain effort to reject the inevitable scorching.

The tallest skull mask of the group was standing in the middle near the fire. He raised his torch , shouting at the others. They raised their torches above their heads. I closed my eyes fearing the blow. The familiar Nevada fear had returned.

III

I was sure the blow was imminent, but it did not come. I pushed through the fear and opened my eyes. The skull maskers had pulled off their masks. My attacker had a bald head, charred tattoos on his neck and colourful face paint. He looked just like a skinhead from a biker gang, like the many who went on to join forces with the Storm Ninjas.

A rage welled up inside me. I gritted my teeth. This was not right. Like the attack on Richardson, it was unwarranted. I directed all my anger against my attacker, thrusting my head towards him with teeth bared, viciously trying to break free. But his eyes were wild, curious, smiling almost, like he harbored no ill-will towards me.

Instead of attacking me, he turned with some of the other attackers and brought fire to the skull masker in the middle of the room. A struggle escalated into a frenzied fight with a skull masker literally burning to death. Some-one set Maya free. In turn, Maya set me free, and we set the others free. By this time, the room was engulfed in flames, and we raced out through the falls.

"Come this way!" Maya was ahead of us, her torchlit face vaguely visible. We followed close behind, careful not to overstep the tree branch in the darkness. The heat from the inferno eased off as we got further away, and the jungle's heat was now more tolerable.

After carefully navigating across bridges and stairs we entered another crack in a tree which led to a room. The torch was placed in the middle of the room, casting a glow on our faces as we recovered. The skull masker that nearly attacked me was standing next to Maya, his mask discarded somewhere along the way.

"What the hell was that?" I yelled, pointing at the man. "We were nearly burned to death back there!"

"You are safe," the man said. "We were there to pro-tect you."

"Could have fooled us," Fathom said. "You nearly burned us all."

"We are Uriah. We are friends," he said. "I am Keon."

"If you are friends, you sure have a funny way of greet-ing folks," Cabell said. "What happened back there?"

"We are friends. Many Uriah are not friends. Some of my tribe want to kill foreigners, like you. But they are evil. My group is not evil. We saved you. We are not violent against the Uri. We like the Uri. We want peace between all."

"Are you a dissenting group from the Uriah?" Cabell asked.

Maya nodded. "Many Uriah do not understand the Uri. But we understand."

"So the Uriah are overall a non-violent crowd," Cabell said, "but a fraction of the lot are turning the whole batch sour. And the Uri are...friendly?"

"Uri will hurt no one," Maya said. "They are all good. They are peaceful."

"So can we speak to the Uri and straighten all this out?" Fathom asked. "We really need to find the ship and get out of here. This is insane. And...where is Myles?" We looked around. Myles was nowhere to be seen.

"Myles?" I cried, panicking. Then the man from before approached me.

"You can relax. We'll get him. We always get our men." My racing heart began to calm. My apprehension and anger toward this man was misleading. His power seemed to shine through his rugged appearance. His words carried conviction. I could see the warrior within him beaming at me.

"We will win all of Uriah, someday," he said. "The path for future is peace for all. We will make it happen. Progress is slow now. But we are winning smaller battles. Now, rest. We will leave to find your friend. At daybreak."

We rested for a few hours. The light from the cracks in the tree began to grow. When it was safe to leave, we moved through the crack, and began on the path back to find Myles.

After a good half hour, we were back at the tree, and it was burning wildly. If Myles had not escaped, there was no way he'd still be alive. And his chances of escape were not much better than our own. Defeated, we paused to consider another plan.

The spears took us completely off guard. They flew from the surrounding bushes. Had our ambushers been waiting for us to return? We tried to see a way out, but there was none. We were surrounded.

◄

We must have looked ridiculous being marched along with our arms tied behind our backs. The expressionless figures with painted faces and sharp spears directed us across jungle branches and bridges and up tree stairs.

We walked over a network of plateaus. There were huts stacked with water jugs, bowls of fruit, and spears. Figures with leafy clothes watched us from inside. Over time, these huts became a city built high up in the jungle.

We passed through a bustling waterfall flowing over a tree trunk,and entered a big circular room with wooden tables lined with fruit. There were more figures eating and speaking in a foreign language. They became silent. At the far wall, water was flowing over a much wider opening that appeared to be a window to the village of huts outside.

A woman sat in a wooden chair at the end of a long table. When approached on the right side of the table by one of our guards, she gestured towards our captors. We stopped. She addressed us in a foreign language. We said nothing. Maya responded in their language, then spoke to us.

"They want to know," said Maya, "why has Uri sent you to spy on them?"

"There was a pause, then Cabell spoke up.

"We are...humans...from far away. We are not the Uri."

Another pause, then the woman at the table spoke to Maya, who translated again. "She asks why. Why do you spy from Uri?"

"We are not Uri," Cabell said, "we are from far away." He paused. "We want peace for all. We want both Uriah and Uri to be at peace."

Again, the woman at the table spoke. Then, a scared look passed over Maya's face. "She says, Uri cause problems in jungle, cause death, why do you do this? You must pay."

The man who had saved us from the fire attack spoke up, and he sounded very mad.

"We don't mean harm" Cabell said. "We just want to go back...to where we're from."

Maya spoke again, then relayed the message again. "She says that you must be Uri. Or outsiders. You do not belong here. You must be jailed."

IV

"Just hold on," I said. "We haven't done anything to you. We just want to leave here!" One of the guards pushed his spear up close to my face.

The guards spun us around and marched us back through the waterfall. My face was hot. The injustice of it made me want to grab a spear and attack one of the guards.

We passed over a new bridge. There was a movement from the bushes on a branch adjacent to the bridge. One of the guards yelled, either in anger or giving an order, I couldn't tell.

The guards raised their spears, shouting, only to be cut off by a barrage of arrows from a higher branch. It was a trap.

Keon kicked one of the guards, who fell back against another. "Go," he yelled, and we all ran back across the bridge the way we'd come. I looked back in time to see Keon barely dodge a spear. He picked it up and cut the bridge vine. The vine disconnected and one side of the bridge dropped. Some guards tumbled off and some desperately held on for their lives. We had more time.

We edged along a branch and stumbled across another bridge. Maya led us to an open plateau. We stopped for a moment to catch our breath. Soon after, Keon stumbled out onto the plateau and dropped the spear he'd taken earlier.

"Cut me free," he said, and Maya cut the vine linking his hands together. He did the same for her, and they cut the rest of us free.

"We have little time," Keon said. "The Uriah have many soldiers."

"Can you take us to the Uri?" Cabell asked.

Keon nodded. "I can, but the path is long, and we have to go fast."

"We have no choice," I said. "Let's go."

❧

We spent days travelling through the jungle. It all looked the same to me, but Maya and Keon said they knew the path well. Many times, we were approached by the same tiger-like creature that had chased me, but Keon turned it away with broad sweeping gestures.

Further down into the jungle, it became darker. Moss was more prevalent. One old tree was completely covered in the stuff. Keon led us through an opening in the tree to a flat piece of wood. He pulled a stick out of his leafy suit and pushed it into the wood. It opened. We moved through the threshold.

It was dark and humid inside. We walked along a wall until Keon asked us to stop.

"It's a long way down," he said. "You take the leaf, place it around your hand, and slide down. Be slow at first, then fast. Don't let go. It's important, do not let go."

"This isn't very safe," Fathom said.

"How far down is it?" Cabell asked.

"It's far," Keon said, "but leaves will protect you. I will go first, to show you. Wait before going."

"What exactly is—" Cabell began, but he was interrupted by the sound of Keon sliding down what I could only assume was a vine.

One by one we followed. I went last. I reached the bottom with a splash. Surprised, I sank below the water, before I doggy-paddled to the surface. It was much cooler down here.

A torch flickered beside a wooden door like the one above. The reflection of the torch glowed in the ripples of the water all around the room. The others waited along the side of the room next to the door . I swam ashore. Keon unlocked the door, and we stepped outside onto a new wooden plateau.

It was dark and murky. Torches were attached to huge

trees continuing into the distance. They were perfectly mirrored in the glassy water below.

A foul, ashy smell reminded me of the smoke from earlier. Keon walked around the back of the tree we'd dropped down from. He returned pulling a small boat by vine, and directed us to jump inside. Maya was fascinated with the water.

The ride through the trees was eerie. We passed board-walks built around trees and docks for fishing. A few had doors and people—presumably, the Uri—sat watching us. Some were smoking. The smoke rose upwards, between the trees.

The path became more obstructed by fog as we continued, and much colder. We had entered the storm, although it was of mild intensity. I shivered.

"Where are we going?" Cabell asked.

"You will meet Graeme," Keon replied. "Our leader. He is really chill, you will see."

We reached three trees with boardwalks. Keon docked the boat, and we jumped ashore. We walked around the tree and continued. The entire area was a big boardwalk.

Above, there were huts made of straw and wood. We continued up a stairway to new level, eventually making it to a hut. We exited on a wooden overhang much like a balcony. It was overlooking a collection of houses lit by torches and surrounded the water. It looked like a small outport fishing community.

Next to us, there was a man sitting on a chair smoking. When he saw us, he stood. He was much taller than any of the other figures we'd seen here. He had black, greasy hair, and the familiar leafy clothing.

"Finally, we meet," the man said.

"You were expecting us?" Cabell asked.

"Of course, my friends. There isn't much I don't know of. You're the folks that fell from 'heavens,' eh? What are you wearing? This is your clothing? Strange." We had long since removed our winter coats. Ironically, we would have loved to have them back now.

"Who are you?" asked Fathom.

"Graeme here, your local Uri leader."

"Well, thanks." Cabell said. "It's great to speak to someone sensible for a change."

"Of course, look, we're not against outsiders like the Uriah. I mean, we're careful who we let in but…we are pretty good at judging character. And we don't blindly worship some ridiculous 'sun god.' We're much more sensible than that." He bent over to pick up a joint and smoked it.

"What kind of joint is that?" I asked.

"This? Oh, this is truly a miracle. Want to try some?"

"I'm good," I said, shivering.

"Not a chance," Cabell said, turning away almost repulsed.

"You never know, you might like it," Graeme said.

"We call it the Atavika 'lief,'" he continued, picking it up and turning it around in his hand. "This is one of the greatest blessings bestowed upon our people. In fact, it's been around since the very beginning. If it weren't for this 'lief here, we'd probably still be lost up there in the clouds with the Uriah, worshiping some ridiculous false god." He took a long puff, then exhaled. "It's powerful stuff. It'll warm you up really quick."

"That's great, but is there a washroom around here?" Cabell asked.

"A washroom?" Graeme replied. "Oh, you mean...I see. Just use the ocean."

"This is an ocean?" I said, looking down below at the water.

"For the most part, yes. I mean, there are areas where there is ice, like in the Fallen Sky, but other than that, it's an ocean that goes on and on."

"The Fallen Sky...do you mean the storm?" said Cabell. "The white mist from the sky?"

"Yes, that's it."

"How has this storm not permeated the jungle? How is it only in certain areas?"

"The jungle protects us. It always has. We worship the jungle, not as a god but as a physical entity. We quite literally worship the Atavika 'lief, which we smoke in our ceremonies. It protects us from the harshness of the Fallen Sky, an area that was once jungle before the great fire."

Graeme took a long drag on his joint. "Are you sure you don't want a puff?" He held it out for us.

Cabell took it, not to smoke, but to study it. We stared blankly at him. He looked like he was connecting a giant puzzle in his mind.

"This is really curious. The chemicals in this plant must have an adverse effect on the storm."

"Well, the 'plant' as you call it, protects us when we have to cross the Fallen Sky, which we usually avoid, as the other side is Uriah territory. But that's exactly where you want to go, isn't it? That's where your 'ship' is."

Each one of us stared at him for a moment.

"The ship?" Cabell said. "You know where it is?"

"Of course," Graeme said. "Your ship fell right on the border between Uriah and Uri territory. We were able to hide it before the Uriah found out about it, but given their intelligence forces, the secret won't last forever.

"We have to get to the ship," said Fathom. "It's the only way for us to get home. Please, take us there."

"Of course," Graeme said. "We'd be happy to. But if you're going to pass the Fallen Sky, you're going to need to smoke some of this," he said, holding out the Atavika 'lief. "This is the only thing that will keep you from succumbing to the Fallen Sky."

We looked at each other. Cabell was quite obviously not at all interested in this, but we all felt that Graeme spoke the truth. It was the only way out.

"We'll do what we have to do," said Cabell.

"Excellent. We're preparing a smoking ceremony soon. Before that, feel free to look around.

V

We crossed the community's boardwalks. Keon explained that he was originally of the Uriah, but had defected as the Uriah had become increasingly religious and oppressive over the years. Although they were peaceful, there was a radicalized group that regularly attacked the Uri. This was the same group that had tried to burn us. In many ways, the radicalized Uriah were like the Storm Ninjas.

"The power of the Uri is much stronger," he said. "We have better, stronger weapons. Our only disadvantage is…we don't attack. Only defend. The Uriah always know when the attacks will happen. We only attack when one of our own is in trouble. We attacked to save you."

I remembered the attack on the bridge. Of course. They were the ones that distracted the guards.

"You saved us," I said. "With the arrows."

"Yes."

"These are your preferred weapons? I have not shot one in years."

"Would you like to?"

"Yes, I'd love to."

With that, Keon led us through another waterfall gateway to an area which was enclosed by trees, torches, and boarded walls covered in moss. Two big waterfalls fell down from high above. A giant bird easily four times taller than me swooped down next to me, giving me a start.

"Relax," Keon said. "These are the Tal, they are friends. They help us. Like sentries they keep us safe."

Keon lifted a wooden lid covered in moss and pulled out a bow with a case of arrows. He handed it to me and gestured towards a torch on the wall. I lined up and took a shot. The familiar stance brought back memories of the archery we'd set up in Nevada. I hit the target dead on. I looked back at Keon, who was smiling with admiration.

"You are very good," he said. "We could use your skill."

I blushed.

"Much of our life here is peaceful," Keon said. "Uriah does not know of this area. They attack us in other parts of the jungle. Your skill could help us defend other Uri strongholds. With aim like that, you could save many lives."

I laughed at the idea. But I was smitten at the compliment.

"You may keep this bow," he said. I refused but he

insisted. "You have a warrior's spirit. You may someday need it." I thanked him for his sweetness and accepted the gift. "Now, we must head back to the ceremony."

A fire blazed on a dock in the middle of the community. All occupants had exited their huts and were smoking by their homes all around us.

Graeme was standing next to the fire. He greeted us with a smile. Sitting on a log next to him, was Myles.

"Thank God you're alive," I said. Myles grinned at me with stoned eyes.

"Bailey! Just think'n about you. Here, have some Atavika 'lief, this is fine." I took the joint and smoked it. The others were hesitant to, but Graeme insisted it would protect them from the storm. The drug grew a warmth inside me that buzzed me unlike anything I'd ever smoked before.

"The Uri saved me after the fire," Myles said. "And man, do they have some setup here. They're free to do what they want all day. It's sweet. I wouldn't mind stay'n here myself."

"That's great," said Cabell, "But I, for one, am getting more than a little homesick, and I've needed to use the washroom ever since we first encountered that homeless guy and his ship."

I remembered Hylotz and the photo I'd taken of him. It seemed like a longshot, but I pulled out the photo and passed it to Graeme. "Have you ever—"

"This guy," Graeme said, "is incredible!"

"You *know* him?" Cabell asked.

"Damn right I know him! Mind-blowing dude. He introduced us to the Atavika 'lief! Without him we'd probably still be Uriah, climbing up the jungle, stupidly worshipping the sun. We're so grateful to have met him. He taught us to speak outside of the Uriah, he taught us so much!"

"His name is Hylotz," Cabell said. "He came from the ship that took us here."

"Where is he?" Graeme asked.

I laughed. "Now there's a question."

"We don't know," Cabell said. "But we're trying to find out. We think he might be at our home."

"Ah yes, your home," said Graeme. "Well, if we can help you get there, we will. In fact, the boat will soon be here to take us across the Fallen Sky." He produced several more Atavika 'liefs for us. "Take these. We may need to smoke more later."

The boat arrived shortly, and we all jumped in. As Graeme and Keon rowed us through the darkness, the frequency of tree trunks grew sparser as the mist grew thicker. The familiar cold of the storm was setting in, yet the warmth from the Atavika 'lief was so strong, it seemed to protect us.

The journey was long. I'd not been out in the storm more than an hour since…Nevada. I shivered at the memory.

After several hours, the storm began to fade again. The massive trees returned. We reached an area with trunks that had stairs ascending, lit by torches. The boat approached an island of moss, which was just a gigantic dead tree stump.

We climbed onto the island. Graeme and Keon walked to the middle of the island and brushed loose moss off several big leaves. They tossed the leaves aside, revealing our ship nestled in a small pool of water.

"I've never been so happy to see such a piece of technology in all my life," Myles said.

"You and me both," I said. We pressed up against the doors and they opened. It didn't appear to be damaged.

"We can't thank you enough for all you've done for us," Cabell said, thanking Graeme, Keon and Maya.

"Can I go?" said Maya. "I want to leave the Uriah." We looked at each other.

"I don't see why not," Cabell said.

There was a wild scream from one of the trees, then a barrage of spears. One hit Keon, and another grazed my head. Keon fell back and rolled, hiding behind an elevated part of the stump. Graeme pulled out his bow and began shooting. The others jumped into the ship immediately. I saw a skull masker shooting from above, and instantly I was triggered. I felt an adrenaline buzz I hadn't felt in years. I pulled out my bow, and took a shot, hitting the skull masker off of the tree. It felt good. I shot another, then another. For the first time in decades, I felt alive again.

"Bailey, get in," Cabell shouted.

"Go!" I cried.

They hesitated only briefly, before the doors closed.

I realized in that moment, protecting Keon and the Uri was more important than the decades I'd spent grieving aimlessly in fearful inaction. The Uri would not lose another soldier. They would gain one.

Who pilots?

Cabell	Maya
Continue reading	Go to Page 92

CABELL PILOTS

"Cabell did it. He saved us from the storm."

"Genius. And we thought it couldn't be done."

"What dedication. What discipline!"

The voices cut through static as the room warmed and the snowy storm dissipated. Through the stony window, the clouds of the storm rolled off into the distance, receding as the chemical spray we had dispersed deflected it. Below, the clouds remained, but since most of the world had elevated to tower heights it did not matter.

"You've finally done it Cabell." The voice replaced the static. "We're promoting you to champion of Earth, although that title isn't quite apt enough. We're having a contest to come up with a better title."

I stepped back from the tower window and sat on my leather sofa. I was happy, wasn't I? Finally, I had achieved what I'd set out to do decades ago. My whole life project had come to an astounding close. I heard a slow, consistent clapping.

"Congratulations." The man's voice came from the left of my leather chair. I turned to see a man with a beard watching me. Hylotz. He was lost in thought. "Of course, there is still a lot of work to be done. That is your specialty, right?"

I stared at him, unsure how to react. This was some sort of dream. But how?

"Lots of work to be done," he said, again. "That's the why. But the how. What about the how?"

He took a joint from his winter coat and lit it, bringing it to his lips. He inhaled. As he exhaled, a green plant grew from his mouth, covering his face and his body. I jumped up and stepped back. The viny green plant would not stop growing. It grew over the walls and out through the window, compacting the small room. I ran to the window looking out over the storm. Below, I could hear the cries of others. I had no choice but to jump.

As I fell back into the storm, its icy cold consumed me again, and I shivered and shook from the dream.

LEBERWURST-57
WITH: CABELL

I

The ship dropped from a dingy gray sky. Below, a forest appeared through the mist. It was boxed in by big gray towers. I turned the wheel left and right to avoid crashing into them. Pulling back on the wheel reduced the speed slightly. We hit the ground hard, sending a puff of dead leaves into the air.

All was silent. Outside, mist surrounded the ship. We opened the doors. The cool, wet air rolled over me. Were we back on earth? It did not seem like it. The towers I had seen during landing were not at all familiar. A red glow of lights could be seen in the distance. They were surrounding the entire forest. "There's the storm," Fathom said, pointing up. There was a trail of white powdery snow where we'd just fallen from.

"I'm happy to be rid of that damn jungle," said Myles.

"This seems like a much more tenable atmosphere," I said. "This is something we can work with."

We walked through the woods, shivering from the cold. I wished I had my jacket, but we had long since discarded our winter clothes in the jungle.

We approached one of the towers I had seen from the ship. Its red lights loomed overhead. It raised high up into the dreary sky. I ran my hand along its cold, smooth surface.

"Steel," I said. "The architecture is advanced. I've never seen any manmade structures this strong."

We continued in the woods. There was an unsettling feeling, like we were being watched.

"Wait," I said. "What's that over there?" There was a web of antlers swaying back and forth. "Looks like we've got company."

The moose stepped out from behind the bushes and stared at us. Fathom stared back at the moose. He was transfixed; lost in thought. Then he frowned with a look of dismay.

"What is it?" Myles asked.

"The moose...just told me where to go."

Myles shook his head. "Fathom man, you're losing it."

"That's impossible," I said.

"It says there is a farm nearby where other animals are being held hostage. It's asking us to save them."

"Give us a break, Fathom," Myles said. "I get that this whole situation is bonkers, but you can't talk to animals, man."

"It says there is a man there, who is dangerous. It says that we should—"

"Seriously, Fathom," I said. "Stop joking around."

"I'm not joking. I'm completely serious."

"Okay so you can talk to animals now," said Myles. "Great."

"Don't you remember the moose back on Earth? It led us to Hylotz's backpack."

With a snort, the moose walked away, and Fathom followed. "What else do we have to go off?"

Myles shrugged at me and hurried after Fathom.

After a long walk through the misty forest, we came to a steel wall fencing us off. It was twice our height, spanning far off into the distance.

"Interesting," I said. "Could this be the farm? Who wants to explore? Fathom? Your moose brought us here."

Fathom shook his head with apprehension. For an emergency responder, he sure was hesitant to act.

"I will," I said.

"Me too," said Myles.

Maya and Fathom helped Myles and I over the fence. On the other side, lines of crops grew in parallel. There was a nearly dilapidated brown barn in the distance, and further beyond there was a white farmhouse.

Myles and I walked towards the farmhouse. While passing the barn, we could see there were cows, chickens and other animals locked inside in cages.

"These conditions are horrid," Myles said.

"Let's try to remain optimistic," I said. "Maybe there is a good reason for it."

Contrary to my optimism, a loud alarm blared through the air, its red lights broke through the mist.

We ran back to the wall, but we could not get over. We were stuck. The others yelled at us, but there was nothing we could do. Drones buzzed through the air and shot at us. I took a hit and fell to the ground with a burning pain in my back. Not long after, Myles dropped beside me.

We were paralyzed by the shots. The drones continued to buzz above us.

An old man approached and tied us up with twine. The tightness strangled my wrists. He dragged us into a barn and dropped us next to a pile of hay while he pulled open a trap door, propping it up with his shotgun. He dragged us to the opening and threw us down into a cellar. It was dim with only a single lightbulb hanging from a wire. As we lay there motionless, the voice of an announcer blared from a radio on a table. The announcer was loud and direct with an authoritative tone, his voice dominating the air waves:

"One dissenter caught in Leberwurst-354, Quarter 2 (-263, 57). You are required to report all dissenters to your supervisors immediately or face imprisonment. You have been watched.

"We appreciate all your work; it is smiled upon and sincerely and severely by the Blessed Guidance as they bring us to higher levels of elation endowing each human life with qualities never before seen only appreciable through years of toil that you happily have embarked upon of your own free will on the day of enlightenment.

"Your break is coming to an end. Please report to the work floor in the next ten minutes or suffer the consequences. We appreciate your cooperation and understanding that no other civilization could thrive at the level of productivity we've reached without your sacrifice."

The radio droned on for a good half hour. Then, the old man returned with the others, one by one, dropping them down next to us. With his balding head and scowl, there was something terrifying about him.

When we were all lying on the cellar floor, the old man climbed down the ladder and took a seat at the table, laying his shotgun next to the radio.

"Explain to me, fools, are you spies?" he said.

We were silent.

"Are you spies?" he demanded, with elevated agitation. I will have you killed if you are. Do you hear me?"

We stayed silent. Petrified.

"The Goddamn Blessed Guidance thinks I'm not running a legitimate operation here, I can damn well tell you I am! It's bad enough this storm has destroyed the year's crops, let alone having the Guidance breathing down my neck."

We were too afraid to speak, so we just listened.

"I'll give you ten minutes to prove you're not with a spy. If you can't prove it, you'll be shot!"

Our silence was horrible. I could feel us all thinking heavily for a good five minutes. I considered a solution. It was scary, but it was the only thing I knew.

"We can help you protect your crops from the storm," I said.

"What?" The man cried. I heard others gasp quietly.

"We have a special 'lief that protects from the storm. It can be smoked. It could be cultivated to—"

The man burst into a genuinely unhinged laughter, almost coughing as he lost control of himself. It was terrifying.

"Special 'lief? Where the hell are you *from* you fool?"

"We are from...a place far away. We came here in a

spaceship. You can have the 'liefs, just please, let us go."

The man paused. I could see his interest growing despite his disbelief.

"Where are these 'liefs, you fool?"

"In my pocket," I said, gesturing to my left side, where I had tucked the Atavika 'liefs that Graeme had given us.

The man walked over and took the 'liefs from my pocket, bringing them back to the table. He pulled out a joint that was already rolled and held it up to my face, accusingly.

"Is this the best you have to offer, fool?" he berated, grabbing his shotgun.

"Smoke it," I replied.

The man paused for a moment. Then he took out a lighter from his pocket and lit the end of the joint.

"If this is a trick, you know you will die before it can kill me," he said.

"It's not a trick," I said, nodding in acknowledgement.

After a few moments ofsmoking, I could see he was feeling the effects of the drug. He became relaxed and placed the shotgun down. In his eyes, it was like he was wondering where we had come from, and whether he could trust us. He came over to me, grabbed me and pulled me to my feet. The others screamed.

"You must think I'm awfully naïve to believe your spaceship story," he barked. "I've heard some tall tales in my day, but this one takes the cake."

"I can prove it," I said. "I'll take you to the ship."

He held my face up to his and stared deep into my eyes. His prying red eyes showed a subtle lack of focus.

It seemed like he was trying to tell if I was being honest. He cursed.

"Fool, you're coming with me."

II

The old man pulled me up through the cellar door and awkwardly dragged me across the farm. The patrolling drones shared the same ominous red-light glow as the surrounding towers from before. He opened the door to the farmhouse and pushed me inside. I fell on the floor onto my side. I squirmed to a sitting stance. There were cupboards lining the walls and a white fridge with scrapes and nicks. Flies buzzed around the sink where dishes were piled nearly overflowing, and there was an old wooden table with a radio in the middle. The same authoritative voice from before droned on, this time it made me feel sick.

"I don't know who the hell you are," he said, "but you're not from around here," He pointed his shotgun at my face. "The Blessed Guidance doesn't smile on foreigners and neither do I. Give me one reason why I shouldn't blow your brains out right here."

I stuttered, squirming to my knees. I could see in his eyes, he was deciding to kill me and the others, and then he would take the 'liefs. His finger slipped over the trigger. There was a ring from his pocket, which momentarily brought a confused look to his face. The effects of the 'lief had dulled his focus. I trembled as he reached down pull his phone out and answer it.

"What? Yeah, no, I haven't seen anything on that dissenter. No. But listen, you got to get down here. I've got something you're going to want to see."

I jumped to my feet and plowed into him with all my might. He yelled out and the shotgun fired. It missed. He struggled against me, but I weighed him down with my body. The drones reacted immediately. Red laser shots blazed through the air outside, closing in on the house. I jumped up and ran. I had little time to react.

There was a knife at the edge of the sink. I grabbed it and dashed away from the sink as another shot rang out. I jumped around the table and ran down a hall, finding a stairway. I ran upstairs. Over the banister I could see that the old man was gaining his footing and turning around.

Shouts came from the direction of the barn. Had the others escaped? At the top of the stairs, I ran for the nearest bedroom. The door was open, and I quickly closed it with my hands. I was barely able to lock it.

I fumbled with the knife I'd grabbed and was able to free myself from my restraints. Outside, someone screamed. I ran over to the window. It was Myles. He'd escaped but was shot down by a laser. The drones turned towards me and approached my window. I pushed a bookshelf across the window to block it.

I searched for another weapon. There was a shotgun in the closet. I didn't know how to use it, but I had to try. There was a loud bang on the door. It was the old man. I held the shotgun tight and ran to the door.

"You're dead!" The old man jiggled the door handle, before a shot rang out, and I jumped back. This was it, I had to act now. I cocked the gun and pointed it at the door, closing my eyes and pulling the trigger, hoping for the best.

The blast recoiled, throwing me back against the hard-wood floor. There was a thump outside the door. I cautiously moved to the hole in the door to see the old man—dead. A dark pool of blood was oozing from his chest.

A drone smashed through a window in the hall and shot at me. I pushed the bed up against the hole in the door. Outside the drones buzzed, swarming around the house.

Not long after there were voices of men outside the house. The drones were not attacking them. The front door to the house opened and I hid in the closet.

"They're shut off," a scratchy voice yelled. There was a noticeable drop in noise from the drones outside. I heard footsteps walking around downstairs. "I'm checking upstairs."

I bit my lip and held my breath.

The footfalls caused the old staircase to creak as the man ascended. Then, another shout from outside. "Get out here!"

The creaks turned into fast footfalls towards the front door. The unknown man had left the house.

I crept up to the window and listened. I carefully pushed the bookshelf aside enough to see outside. They had found the others. They had rounded them up and were taking them away. There was nothing I could do. I crept downstairs and looked out the front door. They were leaving the farm with their new prisoners.

III

Smoke from Atavika 'lief curled around my head. I gazed through the crack of the boarded-up farmhouse window to the misty sky outside. It had been months since we had arrived here, and I'd shot the old man dead. Grief gnawed at me in equal measure to the warm glow of the buzz from the joint.

A greasy long-haired kid appeared at the farmhouse deck and knocked on the door. I swatted and cursed at flies buzzing around my head. I'd tried numerous times to get rid of them, to no avail. Placing my joint in a dish, I grabbed the shotgun and headed for the door.

"Atavika," the boy whispered through the door. I opened it quickly and dragged him into the porch.

"Were you followed here?" I uttered.

"No," the boy cried.

"Where is it?"

The boy craned his neck gesturing at his backpack. I pulled it off his shoulders and searched through it. There they were. Five stacks. I pulled out the bag of the Atavika 'lief and passed it to him. The boy stared at me.

"Well don't just stand there," I whispered. "What? What do you want?"

"I just wanted to thank you," the boy said. "Before you came, the Green Resistance was just a small group of people disgusted with the Blessed Guidance. Now, so many tired workers are turning to this Atavika 'lief to escape the oppressive regime, and they are joining our cause to rebel against the system."

"Just keep quiet about the 'liefs," I said, closing the door on him. I sat back down at the table. I recalled the first day we had arrived here. After the others were taken away, I had locked down the farmhouse. I had scoured all available literature to learn as much as I could about this world.

The old man was a failing farmer who provided for the Blessed Guidance, an oppressive ruling class that lived high up in the towers and had forced most of the population into labor. I had continued in the old man's shoes. Since the Blessed Guidance only communicated by phone, they were unable to tell the difference.

Initially the farm was failing due to the storm, but I had successfully duplicated the Atavika 'lief, which provided a defense from the storm, creating tenable conditions for growth. In the interim, I had formed an alliance with the Green Resistance, an underground retaliatory group against the Blessed Guidance. I had provided them the powerful 'lief, and they had provided me with money to survive.

The others had been forced into manual labor. I had thought about them often, but I could not justify going to find them, it was too dangerous.

The phone rang. I reached into my pocket and looked at the Caller ID. It was a representative for the Blessed Guidance. Cautiously, I answered.

"We've completed testing on the 'lief you provided. This product has the potential to protect Leberwurst from the storm indefinitely. We are astounded by your level of genius. Your work must continue, and we have gladly prepared a spot for you in a local tower, where you can live out your years of servitude in conditions far surpassing that of a farmer. Do you agree to this?"

"I do," I replied. "But regarding my request to have selected local assistants…"

"This is not a reasonable request. Local laborers remain detached from tower servants. You will have colleagues that will be chosen for you, but your request is highly unorthodox."

"I understand," I said.

"Nevertheless, you yourself are a bit of an anomaly. How you have grown this genius from the role of a lowly farmer is...baffling. Yet if you keep your head down and keep up your work, you will continue to be rewarded with the necessities required for your position. Again, this is more than many will ever know."

"I understand," I replied. "Thank you."

I hung up the phone. I stared at myself in the kitchen mirror. My hair had grown long, and I now had a beard. The Atavika 'lief had become a part of me. It was the only way I could relax. I had wanted to leave this place many times. I had returned to the ship but, I was unable to bring myself to operate it. I had hidden it, determined to return the next day and leave, but I could not do it. Something was holding me back.

Now, the prospect of life in the towers was much more pleasing than the stress of farm life. I would have recognition. Colleagues who would understand and respect me. It was more compelling than my isolation at Last Bastion even, where no one understood the value of my work. The radio buzzed to life, interrupting my thoughts.

The three foreigners found on Leberwurst-57 Quarter 1 (35, 18) have been sentenced to death. Their verdict has been a long time coming. The Blessed Guidance have given you much to be thankful for, yet still dissension has become such a problem, we have been forced to take action. We expect that the death of the foreigners will evoke a new age of higher productivity and we welcome it. We wish only to show you how *efficient* you can be when you put your minds to something, and this ambition is wasted upon the dissenters. Going forward, if you are harboring dissenters or foreigners, you will meet an in-kind fate. You have been watched. May the most blessed of all guidance direct you to beautiful toil through diligent longevity.

I paused, taking a moment to stare at myself in the mirror. I was ashamed. I punched the mirror. I had to snap out of it. I had to take some sort of action. They were my friends. I could not let them die. I gritted my teeth and grabbed the shotgun from the table.

IV

I flung the old man's backpack over my shoulder and set out on the path towards the processing plant. Through the Green Resistance, I had learned everything I needed to know about the layout of the factory, which was guarded by drones.

I approached the familiar large rock at the base of a landslide. Pushing it aside, I revealed the small cave I had come for. I pushed the rock back in place. At the back of the cave, there was a stone wall. I knocked on it with in a memorized beat. The wall slid aside, and I was greeted by two Green Resistance soldiers with guns, ready to shoot.

"Cabell, what brings you?" the soldier said relaxing, his dusty face becoming visible as my eyes adjusted to the dim lantern lights.

"I'm infiltrating the factory," I said.

"No way! The drone security is—"

"Look I've thought about it, and I have friends in there that will be put to death. It has to be done."

"It's a suicide mission!"

"It doesn't have to be. I'll need more weapons. Muster up some of the extras. Jex, is the west entrance to the factory still accessible?"

"It is, but—"

"Look I don't want to talk about it, okay? I'm going to do it. After we return, there is no way they will find the underground headquarters. I will under no circumstances lead them to it."

The soldiers looked scared, but they nodded their heads and rounded up several more shotguns and pistols with extra ammunition. They brought me to the west entrance to the factory.

The factory was an old warehouse that at one time was used to store dead animals but had been long since taken out of commission. Dilapidated machinery lay strewn about. The Green Resistance had tapped into an old drainage system in the warehouse that offered an escape for dissenters.

I lifted the grate off, and I quietly propped my head up. After surveying the area, I stepped out and placed the cover back on the drain. I crept to a door which led to a hall, and made my way down it, entering a ventilation system which connected both old and new buildings. Not fun, especially with a bag full of guns.

When I reached the sweatshop, I had to move carefully. The drones prowled with blood red eyes. They flew back and forth along the walls monitoring the workers below. The workers operated along a conveyer line poorly lit by florescent lights.

With the help of the Green Resistance, I had listened in on sensitive recordings of schedules determined by the Blessed Guidance, and I knew my friends would be working on this shift. It was a disgusting job, the slaughter and processing of animals for mass consumption.

I made my way down a ventilation shaft and unlocked a vent door, sneaking into the processing room. From behind a bigger piece of machinery, out of view of the drones, I looked over the faces of the workers in their white suits. Most were unfamiliar, but my eyes landed on a shorter worker. It had to be Maya.

An alarm blasted through the processing area and a red light flashed. A laser shot towards me, but I dashed away and returned fire. A nearby drone fell to the floor. The other drones swarmed in, and I shouted at my friends. They ran to me avoiding the laser fire.

"The bag, guns in the bag," I shouted, while unloading on the swarming drones.

The others grabbed the guns, and soon we were all shooting the drones down. It was not going to be enough, every drone in the factory would be on its way here.

"Quick, we have to get to the door," I screamed and led the others to one of the doors. The door was locked, but a shotgun to the lock quickly fixed that. I busted through the door with the others, and we made our way down a long hallway towards a staircase.

Three drones ambushed us on the stairs, and I nearly took a shot in the shoulder. Myles shot the drone down.

We ran down the staircase with more drones behind

us. We shot open a front door and flew out into the night air. There were more drones ready for us. We had to run along the side of the factory shooting them, until finally we found shelter in the forest.

V

We survived the run to the farmhouse without incident. Once inside, the others collapsed on the kitchen table.

"There's no time," I said, "We've got to go. More drones will be coming!"

The radio blasted to life.

Leberwurst-13 Quarter 4 (22, 09) has been compromised. The dissenters will be killed. Report any unauthorized movement immediately. Searcher drones have been dispatched.

Did they know we were at this farm? No. They were still searching, meaning any drone strike would not be too formidable. But they would be fast. Ten minutes. I reactivated the farm drones and turrets. If they wanted war, they would get it.

"We've got ten minutes before the drones show up," I said. "We have to go. Now."

We made our way across the farm and through the gates, where we were met by an army of attacking drones.

They came slow at first, succumbing to the farm's drones that were buzzing around the periphery. Then they came in full force. We were forced to take refuge in the barn. These were only the first wave of drones, though. The next wave would be much, much worse. After the drone war that ensued, only four of my drones were left remaining. We would not survive the second wave. We had to go.

My phone received a radio signal.

Full attack! Leberwurst-57 Quarter 1 (35, 18)

I undid the locks for the animal cages. I instructed everyone where to run for the ship, and we escaped the farm property just before the second wave of drones arrived. During our run to the ship, we could hear them buzzing in the distance.

We arrived at the same clearing where we had first landed. We all brushed leaves off the ship and jumped inside. My phone blared.

Dissenters identified at Leberwurst-57 Quarter 1 (156, 8), Shoot immediately!

I tossed the phone out onto the ground just before the ship doors closed. Maya jumped in the driver's seat and took the wheel. The ship pulled up off the ground just as the drones arrived. They shot through the windshield, but their blasts were easily deflected off the ship.

As the ship began to spin in connection with the storm, I sighed. I was happy to leave this horrible nightmare behind.

MAYA PILOTS

They yelled at me from above, their spears high in the white air. They chased me down under the bright hot sun until I stood at the edge of a tree branch.

"You aren't like us," they said. "We don't want you here. Go."

My face was hot with anger. They hated me, and I hated them. I turned away from them, gazing into the darkness below, and I jumped.

I hit the water with a big splash. The water was very cool. Light fell from above.

Through the water, there were more faces. Many figures. Feminine. Beautiful. Glowing. Purple and blue. Their arms were locked together with…a man? A big man. He had much hair. His face was flushed red. He was happy.

He smiled at me and unlinked one of his arms. He gestured for me to join them. A dark shadow eclipsed the light overhead. I turned to the bearded man and the women. I followed them.

PART THREE
ONDAS
WITH: MAYA

I

We fell.

Like Tal falling from the sky.

Down down down.

There was a fiery blaze. Out there. Over an endless sea. Reigning like a god. Between sleep and wake.

We were so small.

I felt helpless. I missed the jungle cricket chorus. I missed the monkey dances. I wanted them back.

The sea closed in. Our screams did not stop it.

We smacked into water. Sides opened. Water rushed in. Screams muted. We struggled, but no. I could not make it. I could not swim.

Something tugged me. A soft blurry face. Bright like the sky. Calming the waves of fear. I tried to swim up, but I could not fight sleep.

ᴧ

I coughed. Raspy. Like a dying monkey. Struggling for a last breath. Arms and legs lashing out.

A face stopped my struggle. I forced free. I ran to the light. I fell into water.

"It's okay Maya," said Fathom. "You nearly drowned. We're all here. You're going to be fine. You can calm down."

My heart pounded. Like the drums of the Uriah celebration of God. I stared at him. Light running off the side of his face. Running into the water. Running out to the fiery blaze in the sky. The winds were loud. Cold. The sky was dark. The ocean was black just like the Uri village. But it was not Atavika.

"There's no exit other than the cave's opening," Cabell said. His voice bounced. "Curious, though, the positioning of the rocks suggests someone was hiding out here. And that gigantic red dwarf on the horizon is—unsettling. We're definitely not on Earth."

"No kidding," Myles said. "Can we all agree we've bit off more than we can chew with that goddamn ship?"

"The question is, just what determines where we end up? This navigational technology is way beyond anything we have on Earth. There doesn't seem to be any rhyme or reason to it, yet it appears to be propelling us across massive distances in space."

There was a splash. Myles spun around fast. "What in the sweet mother was that?"

We stared out of the cave. No sound. Only ocean waves. Only angered winds.

"I'm ready to peace out," Myles said.

Cabell sighed "We all are, but our ticket out of here lies at the bottom of that ocean. How are we going to get it? We might be trapped here forever."

Myles groaned. "How the hell did we survive the crash anyway?"

"Didn't you pull me out of the ship?" Fathom said.

"Hell no. Cabell pulled me out."

"I didn't," Cabell said. "I thought that…well, if none of us did, then—"

The water splashed. Creatures dove out at us. Like giant sharks. I screamed. Too late. A creature tackled me to the ground. I tried to move but it locked my hands. The others yelled. It was no good. They had us.

II

The ocean roared behind us. Like the Uriah. Angry for me to leave. We walked up a dark beach. Rocks cut like razor teeth. Wind stung like a hornet's nest. I fell. A sharp pain in my back. Wrists tied. It was our captors. They pushed me back up.

We entered bushes. The leaves jumped out of the way. Like grasshoppers escaping attack. They were black. Like wet soil. They moved with a secret life.

Our captors looked dangerous. Sharp spikes on their backs. Pointy noses. Shiny skin like a fish hiding in the ocean.

We walked long through dense bush. We were in a forest now. Strange swaying dark trees. The ocean roar was gone. We walked for so long. The harsh winds froze us. The trees shielded us some. But that made the freezing pain worse. I never knew this type of horror before. I wished for death by tiger.

After many steps we stopped at a fire. I stepped back. The fire scared me. Ever since the great fire in Atavika. It always felt scary to me. But the trees were tall here. They swayed above in the wind. They offered some protection.

A shark man disappeared into a cave. He returned with a man in old, hooded clothing and clunky glasses. The man was smoking something. The two spoke by gestures.

"Humans," he yelled with anger. "Where the hell did you come from?"

We were silent. Could we trust him?

"Well it's really quite something," Cabell said, "there was a ship—"

"The ship? Where is it!" the man shouted. We went silent again. "H-Hylotz is behind this. I know he has the ship. Where is he, Goddamnit? Where is he?"

Cabell paused, surprised. "Well, the ship unfortunately met an untimely fate with the ocean…"

"Shut up!" The man yelled. He stomped his foot in anger, dropping his glasses on the ground. I jumped back in shock. He searched for the glasses. "Hylotz will pay for what he's done! N-no one steals from Duncan and lives through it! You'll r-rot until we find the bastard! Onda," he gestured to the shark-like men. "Take them to the i-ice caves! They'll die there f-for all I care!"

Our captors marched us through the forest. No more trees. It was colder. A deep cold like I never knew. The ground changed. Slippery. No more trees. Very strange. Was this ice?

We reached a rock on the ground. After much time. The Onda pulled the rock aside. Stairs led down into darkness. The Onda took torches and forced us into the opening. Each step into the ground was colder. In time the walls turned to ice. Sharp spikes threatened us from above. Were Onda hiding in the ceiling, ready to attack with spears? Our captors opened another rock door and pushed us into a small cave. They locked the door in place. We were prisoners in this horrible cold cave.

III

"Ain't this is about as far from sanity as you can get," said Myles. "I'd kill that idiot for his smoke."

"Just what did that man—Duncan—What did he say about Hylotz?" said Fathom. "How the hell could he know Hylotz if Hylotz is on earth? I mean, if we really aren't on Earth, because this sure doesn't seem like it."

"It's upsetting for sure," said Cabell. "One would have to assume this is some crazy simulation on Earth, if it's not actually another planet. And our technology is nowhere near the level of such a simulation so this *must* be another planet. But why would Duncan give a damn about Hylotz?"

"I want to go home." I said.

"I second that," Myles said.

"Look everyone, calm down," Cabell said. "There must be a way out of here. Everyone, try to break free from your restraints."

We struggled much. I tried for a long time, and I escaped the trap. My knot was not so tight.

"I am free," I said.

"Oh man, seriously?" Myles said.

"Yes. I am free."

"Free us," Fathom said.

I tried to free them. But I could not. The knots were too hard for my tiny hands.

"Never mind that Maya. Feel around the room. Can you open the door?" Cabell said.

I checked the walls. Cold and slippery. But there was no escape. It was hard to feel through shaking. I felt a door, but it was solid stone.

"The door is locked. Walls cold," I said.

"Maya, you're doing good, just try hitting the walls with your fist. How hard are they?" Cabell said.

I did as asked. The walls were very hard. Except one space. It felt empty like hollow of tree.

"One space feels empty," I said.

"Maya, try to hit the space with all your force!" Cabell said.

I tried this. It did nothing. "I can't break it."

"Show me where it is, Maya."

I took his hand. Brought him to the wall. He hit it hard. Nothing at first. The others joined in. There was a cracking sound. They hit harder. Then there was a break. The wall broke apart and everyone cheered.

"Push the ice away," said Cabell.

There was much noise. They cleared a space.

"Maya, can you fit in there?" Myles said.

I pulled myself into the hole. It was big enough.

"Excellent. Be very careful and go slowly. See if you can find an escape." Cabell said.

I crept through on my hands and knees. My body was in much pain from the cold. Soon I came to a bluish light. It was at the end of the opening. It was brighter here on the other side with many ice spikes high above. The light bounced around a cave. Far above I could see its source. It was the fiery ocean god leading me to freedom.

▲

The cave was bright and beautiful. If I climbed high enough, I could escape. But without the others. Should I leave them?

One wall was a deep blue. The ice was smooth. White circles of light rose behind the wall. I returned to it many times, placed my hand against the ice. I imagined what could be out there. Was there a way home? Back to the jungle? I remembered my home. I wished for it badly.

I saw something through the ice. In the water. In the distance. It was watching me. A bluish figure. Blurry. The reflection reminded me of my Atavika friend. Many times, I saw her reflection in a bucket of water, when we gathered water for the Uriah. I liked her a lot. Then one day, the Uriah separated us. I never saw her again. I missed her.

At first, this figure was shy, and it stayed far away. But it came closer. I felt a longing to know it. Like my longing to return home. But, more than that, I felt a new warmth. A longing to know something like myself.

Then, one time, it came very close. It matched my hand. I could feel warmth through the cold ice, like waves of heat from the jungle's sun. Beautiful green eyes. Bright blue, smooth skin. Soft, gentle hands and swift strong legs.

And the voice started. Slow at first. But then stronger. *Who are you?* The voice was from the creature. But there was no sound. Somehow, it came through the ice, like waves washing over me. I asked myself it the same thing. Who am I?

The questions continued. We spent more time together.

"Are you from the ocean?" the voice said.

"I am from the jungle."

"Why are you here?"

"A ship brought me here."

"Are you a friend of the bearded man?" I paused at this. I remembered the man who taught us how to smoke in Atavika. I remembered his friendliness.

"Yes. He taught me many things. In the jungle. I miss the jungle. My friends are very cold. We need to escape this cave."

"There are many of us. We may be able to help. What is your name, small one?"

"I am Maya."

"You are a very beautiful creature, Maya. I am Onesia. I live with many other Onda like me, in the ocean."

Onesia's voice was soft and caring. We shared a similar curiosity for that which we did not know.

I told Cabell and the others about her. They thought I was crazy, but we continued our talks.

During one of our talks, Many Onda appeared. They looked up and down at me. I stared at them, imagining. Then the voices washed over me like a flood of rain in a storm.

"She's so tiny."

"Where could she be from?"

"Was the bearded man, right? Are there really other worlds?"

"I don't know if we should help her. What if she is a spy for Duncan?"

"But her thoughts appear innocent. And she knows of the ship. And she can speak through the cold."

"If she knows the bearded man, maybe she can return him?"

We must at least try to help her."

Over time they appeared with a larger object in their arms. They pushed it into the ice. I stepped far back. They swam back. Then swam in fast. They pushed the ship into the ice. Many times, they did this. Then one time, they burst through. Water went everywhere. It came up to my feet in the cave. It knocked me back. I stood up and saw our ship surrounded by the Onda.

▲

I led Onesia to the hole. "I am here with new friends," I said, through the hole.

"They are tied," I told Onesia. She nodded, lifted herself up and pushed through the hole. Her hands were bigger than mine, she could untie them one by one. They were free. Slowly, they crawled through the hole. They were barely able to fit.

"Maya, I can't believe you saved us," Myles said. Water was coming up to his knees.

"I am good at these things," I said. Cabell laughed. They all bowed to their savours, the Onda women.

"This is amazing; these women are the Onda as well? They are beautiful," Fathom said. "But they don't speak, how did you convince them to rescue us?"

"They speak, through here," I said, pointing at my head.

The others stared blankly at each other.

"You know what, I believe it. Given everything that's happened thus far, I one-hundred percent believe it," Cabell said.

"Me too," Myles said.

"Well please tell them thank you," Cabell said. The water was up to his waist. "The only problem we have is this water, and there aren't any exits."

"I guess that's our cue to leave," Myles said, walking up to the ship. He opened the ship door. Water spilled out. "I suggest we get the hell out of here fast. I can imagine better fates than drowning in a cave. Let's throw the dice on this beast."

We all walked into the ship. We jumped inside.

"Will you bring the bearded man back to us?" Onesia asked.

"I will try, if we can find him," I thought back.

The ship doors closed. The Onda women stood around us with curiosity.

"There's only one problem," Fathom said. "How do we know we're not going to crash into the wall when we start this thing?"

"I really never thought about that," Myles said.

"It could be pretty dangerous," Fathom said. "This thing is pretty damn unpredictable." The water was up to the glass.

"Well, we better figure something out soon," Cabell said. "The ship is airtight, but the cave is filling up fast. I'm not sure if it can withstand it."

I looked at Onesia. She looked back with big beautiful green eyes. She knew what I was thinking. Then the ship bobbed. We felt weightless. Through the windows of the ship, we could see the Onda pulling us through the water.

"Woah," Myles said.

"Incredible. It looks like our friends are saving us

again," Cabell said.

The ship moved forward, faster as the water came up over the edge of the glass. The blue light from above faded. We crossed the hole in the ice wall and moved out into the big dark sea.

IV

Down, down, down.

We moved down into the dark ocean, away from the ice above. At first, it was scary—the ship shook like when we first fell into the ocean. It felt like we would fall apart. But the Onda were strong. We soon felt a sharp tug, the ship felt warmer, it moved with great force.

"Ocean currents," Cabell said. "They can reach velocities of up to 1.5 metres per second. Perhaps we will go faster, with help from our friends here."

Fish appeared through sky light—an incredible sight. Beautiful blues, reds, pinks, browns and yellows, there was nothing I have ever seen like it.

We moved upwards. An ocean reef appeared, a great rocky mass, a cave filled with coral appeared. We moved through it. Many beautiful creatures were hiding in the coral. They poked their heads out to say hi, like the sneaky animals hiding behind bushes in the jungle.

We exited the cave into the coral reef that was a giant maze of more caves. Onda women peeked out at us from the caves.

"This is beautiful," I thought, to Onesia.

"This is our home," she replied.

We moved further up, But and the water grew colder. A white snow, like over our jungle, was in the water. We entered, and it became freezing, dangerous, painful. It felt like when I flew the ship.

We could only see white, the cold continued to get worse. I felt a wave of change come over me, and I felt it in the others. Not like before, more closely. I felt how they felt the same. I felt connected to them. I reached out to Onesia. My mind branched off into many paths. I felt my thoughts grow stronger, clearer, coalescing with the thoughts of others.

"What is this?" I asked.

"A great magic," said Onesia. *"From the heavens."*

There was no pain. My mind felt light, like I could move anywhere. I thought of the jungle and felt as if I was back there. I thought of other places untravelled. It felt like I was moving there too. I felt my friends, men and women, many different types, happy together. And I felt my mind change, growing a new strength, growing together with many, growing, and moving great distances, balancing a great power. Onesia spoke to me now, her voice had become different. Like she'd changed as well. She was speaking with her many Onda sisters through the storm. Then she spoke to me.

"Maya, you're a strong one, quite small, yes, but very strong. I can feel you. I can tell from your thoughts where you come from. It's an incredible jungle, and you miss it dearly. You want to return, but you also love to explore, and you're curious about my people.

"The Ondas were once a strong and proud race. Male and female Ondas lived together in the ocean in harmony. This all changed when this great white storm met our world. At first it was intriguing, as the images and feelings it brought were

celestial; it seemed to connect us to a broader world with greater potential. However, many Ondas got lost in it, and we believe many of them died. It became detrimental to our home, causing us to move to other parts of the ocean to sustain life.

"However, one day a ship just like this one dropped from the storm. From it two men appeared. A bearded man and an older man with glasses. We saved them, like we saved you in your ship when you first arrived. We left them on a beach. At first, they were horribly inept, so we brought them food and helped them build a home.

"The bearded man took a liking to the Onda women. Somehow, he was able to speak to us, and he taught us how to survive in the storm. The older man took a liking to the Onda men. He taught them how to survive on land, and how to build land structures.

"But as the storm grew worse, there came a time when the older man changed. He taught the Onda men that the way to beat the storm was to fight it through strength. To become stronger. To live on land and build stronger settlements against the storm.

"He taught them that women were weak to remain in water. He taught that true strength could only be obtained through pursuits on land. He also became obsessed with finding the ship that they had fallen in.

"The bearded man remained patient and tried to quell this change, but he was unsuccessful, and one day a physical fight broke out between the two. The fight led the bearded man to hide out in caves, and eventually the Onda men grew such a presence on land that the bearded man was forced to leave, with the help of us women.

"The bearded man swam with us to an island unvisited by

the older man. The island was good enough for him to live peace-
fully for a long time. It is this island where we take you now."

Hearing Onesia's thoughts, I felt how beautiful she was. She accepted me as I was. Even though I was different. She did not wish me away. She swam through the water with such ease. I felt a reflection of my own curiosity within her grow, as my mind changed to join hers. I dreamed of joining her diving in the waves, flowing through the many pathways of the storm, reaching out to visit the depths of the Ondas ocean, to many other places, and maybe someday even to visit back home in my jungle. I felt her dream of one day uniting the Onda men and women, I wanted to help.

And then, I felt a new change. The storm fell behind us. I felt as I was before. We began to flow up, my thoughts returned to normal. The ocean god appeared above—a great light in the sky.

V

We stepped out onto the small island. It was burning hot, windy. The sky was blue with a bright light. There was a small hut in the middle of the island. The wind was very bad. We all had to run to the shelter of the hut. It burrowed into the ground, big enough for all of us.

"Looks like someone was living here for quite a while," said Fathom.

"The rocks here in the middle suggest a fire," Myles nodded. "And there's no shortage of fishbones. And look—A pipe. Well well, what do we have here. Matches and black leaves everywhere. What do ya say we smoke some of 'em?"

"Not sure about that," Fathom said. "I mean, could be completely unsafe, we don't know how the body's going to…"

"Oh, come on Fathom. It'll be a laugh. What do ya say, Cabell?"

Cabell sighed. "Fine, whatever. I don't really care at this point."

"Yeah," said Myles. They created a smoke, passed it around. Was it like the Atavika 'lief? I liked that. I smoked it too. It felt amazing. Fathom liked it so much that he kept some.

"Given the climate here it's fair to say we're on a tidally-locked planet," Cabell said. "This section of the planet would be facing the red dwarf we saw earlier, and thus in perpetual daylight."

We looked out through a window in the hut opposite to our entrance. It provided a full view of the ocean. There were black rocks far in the distance.

Cabell pointed. "You can see where day turns to twilight. That's where we landed."

"That's where we met that crazy Duncan dude and his Onda minions," Myles said.

Onesia appeared at the doorway. Behind her, the other Onda women. We all stared.

"What are they thinking, Maya?" Cabell said.

I looked at Onesia and thought, *"are we safe from Duncan's Onda men?"*

"You are very safe." Onesia said. *"They have never been here."*

"We are safe from them," I said.

"Well, that's great, but I don't plan on staying here

much longer," said Myles. "Let's move."

"Where will you go? Will you find the bearded man?" Onesia thought.

"We will try."

"I want to be with you," she thought. In my mind, I remembered the storm, the way her mind felt, her dreams of exploring, her dreams of reuniting the Ondas. Much like mine, I wanted us both to explore. Here, there was no Uriah to separate us.

"Wait," I said. "I want to stay with Onesia."

The others stared.

"If you want," Cabell said.

I stared at Onesia. *"Do you want to come and explore with us?"* I thought to her.

"To go would be fine, although I could stay," she thought.

"Onesia wants to join," I said. "She wants to explore." I looked at Onesia. *"Do you want to drive this ship?"* I asked.

"Yes, very much," she said.

"She wants to drive," I said.

Cabell paused, thinking. "You know, I guess it doesn't really matter who pilots, because wherever we end up...it seems awfully random."

"I'd really like to know what it's like to pilot," said Myles.

"Well, honestly, either of you could pilot at this point. We'll figure it out when we get to the ship.

Fathom stepped out through the doorway to head for the ship. "Oh no," he shouted. "The ship is floating away with the tide!"

We ran to the entrance. The ship was far away. The

Onda women were gone.

"We've got to swim to it," Cabell said. "Go, quickly."

We ran to the ship. Into the water. But I could not swim. I yelled at the others. My arms struggled against the waves. I felt myself go under. I was drowning. I felt myself drift to sleep. Like when we first arrived.   But I did not sleep. Instead, I sank. I breathed in the water. It filled me. I moved my arms. I could still swim. I swam again. I was above the water again. I swam to the ship with the others. We all held on.

"What happened?" said Cabell. "We thought we lost you."

"I fell underwater," I said. "But I did not drown."

"As did I," said Fathom. "The water filled my lunges, but I didn't drown. Could it have anything to do with what we smoked?"

"Curious," said Cabell. "But we must decide. Who will stay and who will go?"

"I will join Onesia either way," I said.

Who pilots?

Onesia   Myles
Continue reading   Go to Page 117

ONESIA PILOTS

The cold of the storm kept me locked in a floating iceberg. As it melted, I fell deeper and deeper into the water. The water was occupied by many of my fellow Onda women and men. The waves stretched my mind out over a vast distance, resonating with the lives of many Onda.

Somewhere out there, I could see an old friend. That old, bearded man, what gentle eyes he had. His warmth lighted up my soul. I could feel his smile forming from my lips. Like the first day, when he arrived, when Onda men and women lived together in peace. His smile was like a new beginning. He whispered that all would be happy once again.

I reached out to hug him, but somewhere, in the vastness of space, something changed. A darkness overcame me. The same darkness that divided our people. Everything went black.

ONDAS
WITH: ONESIA

I

The wind jolted us back and forth as we fell to the ground. Our direction was all off; I couldn't make a level landing. It was terrifying. We hit the ground so hard the front of the ship became stuck, cracks in the ice spread out like ripples across the sea.

We pried the doors open and spilled out. It was freezing.

"This is strange," said Cabell, "What a familiar ambiance. Are we on the same planet?"

We walked around in near complete darkness, but I knew immediately where we were. It was the great ice sheets that I'd explored as a child. *"This is Ondas,"* I said to Maya. *"We are still on Ondas!"*

"Onesia says we're back on Ondas."

"This can't be right. This hasn't happened before," Cabell said.

In the distance, through the bluster of the storm, several figures approached, including one with a lantern. Upon their approach, I knew it was the Onda men. With them was Duncan, in his puffy black coat and hood. His presence sent me into the same revolt I'd experienced in the cold dream.

"We have to get away, it's Duncan!" I thought to Maya. But it was too late.

"Thought you could escape, eh?" Duncan said. We remained quiet, ready to run, but saw that we were trapped in. There were many Onda men approaching us from all sides, closing in on us in a circle.

"You w-won't be escaping this time, my friends," Duncan said and pulled back his hood. His cold blue eyes focused on the ship. "How delightful of you to bring the s-ship right to me!"

As he approached, the Onda men captured each of us, holding our hands back. Duncan paused for a moment, then removed a small, wrapped collection of black leaves from his jacket and touched it against the candle at the inside of the lantern. He inhaled, his pupils growing and glowing in satisfaction.

"Let us go," Maya screamed.

"What is your problem dude?" Myles asked.

"My problem," he said, again inhaling the joint, "is you've been keeping my sh-ship from me. Do you know how much power this ship has? It very well may have the power to take us away from this cursed storm!" Again, he inhaled. "And conversely, it can shipwreck you on a planet like *this*, stuck with a blundering fool."

"Hylotz," Cabell whispered, under his breath. Then he spoke up. "You and Hylotz were stuck on this planet?"

"That thief," Duncan said, spitting on the ground. "Hylotz was an idiot. He w-wasted his chances of using this ship to advance us beyond the storm. We could be on the way to reaching out to other civilizations and establishing s-solid alliances, but instead he's used the ship as his own personal limousine, using it to take him wherever he wants. Our Marzanna village was burgeoning before he arrived. Before the ravaging storm. He did nothing but steal from us! He can r-rot in hell for all I care, wherever the h-hell he is."

"So you're going to leave us here?"

Duncan flicked his smoked joint to the ground. "Just like Hylotz did when he found the ship and left me here, alone with the Onda. Now in the interest of avoiding losing this ship again, you *will* be stepping aside."

The Onda pulled us back from the ship as Duncan opened the door and stepped into the driver seat.

"Well don't just stand there," he yelled at his minions. "Free the sh-ship!"

Many Onda men pulled against the ship to try to free it from its crater, but it was stuck too deep. Duncan shouted at them until he became so angered, he screamed.

"Oh, give it a rest, back up!" He shut the door. We stepped back as the ship ignited with a green-metallic glow, sparking to life. There was a very soft hum as the metal pushed tight against the ice, at first to no avail, but then the cracks across the ice spread like wildfire.

By the time everyone realized what was happening, the fragmented cracks were splitting ice miles away, and in a massive blast, the ice fractured and sent us all into the water with the ship.

▲

As we submerged in the icy cold water, several other Onda women who I'd called to appeared below. A mad fight ensued between Onda women and men, each of us struggling to break free. I could see our new friends being pulled deep down below. Strange creatures, they could not breathe underwater, they would surely die.

An Onda man grabbed me and pulled me back. I punched him in the head and swam downwards. The only escape now was down. Up surely would be dominated by angry Onda men. I sadly realized there was no way to help our friends.

I thrusted my arms through the water as fast as I could. Despite their strength, the swimming of an Onda man could not rival the swimming of an Onda woman. I evaded the Onda men and swam much deeper down into the ocean. I swam through cracks in coral that led me to a glowing bright orange, volcano caves, I'd remembered from my childhood. It was much hotter here, but Onda men hated the harsh warmth, preferring the cool dark, like that of Duncan's dusky caves.

When I was sure I was safe from detection, I sent out a nearby telepathic sonar to my Onda women, a few of whom I found nearby. We searched for Maya and the others, but we could not find them. In a last-ditch effort, we dove down into the volcanic cracks deep below, braving the scorching hot conditions. To our surprise we found the ship there, with the door open. Duncan was nowhere to be seen.

We pulled the ship up, up through an underwater cave which led to the open chamber of an inactive volcano. Pulling to the surface of the water, we were able to push it out of the water and onto the ground.

Through the opening of the volcano there was a long,

white, cylindrical column of the storm. I knew that I could reach greater distances by thinking through the storm, so I lay down with my head in the storm.

I could hear Maya's thoughts and I could sense her distance from me. She was alive. I could see the others but could not reach them through the storm. I alerted as many Onda Women as possible to go for Maya, as Maya searched for the others, and direct them to the volcano.

Maya finally arrived with the others. She ran into my arms and kissed me. *You saved me again!"* She thought. *"I love you. I want to stay with you forever."*

"I love you too," I said. *"You can stay as long as you want."*

"Thank you for saving us Onesia," said Cabell, "we are truly indebted to you. But it was strange, how were we able to breathe underwater for so long?"

I thought back to the bearded man and his journeys with us, and I realized the answer.

"The 'lief of the bearded man, this 'lief helped him travel with us underwater, and it has let you breathe underwater," I said.

"The 'lief we smoked lets us breathe," said Maya. "Onesia says the bearded man used it. To swim with them."

"Incredible," Cabell said.

Cabell was interrupted by a splash from below. It was Duncan, running to the ship. He punched Maya in the face, and she fell, but she tripped him briefly. We all ran to him as he opened the door.

"Get the hell away!" Myles yelled. Duncan punched him and jumped in the ship. He tried to close the door, but

I stopped him. I pulled him with help from the others and we pushed him out of the ship as the others blocked the door. They jumped inside and Myles took the pilot's seat.

Suddenly, Duncan grabbed me by the throat and strangled my neck, but Maya ran into him with her entire force, causing him to fly back against the floor. Lifting from the ground the ship exited the volcano caves, as the Onda swarmed in and restrained Duncan in his rage.

MYLES PILOTS

Bitter cold winds swirled around me. As the storm eased off, I could see I was holding on to the edge of a cliff. Above me was a figure. My father? He guided the way as we climbed up the perilous surface.

The storm below disappeared to reveal a pleasant mountain village, shopkeepers opening their businesses. Children playing in the streets. By all accounts it was a lovely scene.

The figure above turned down to face me. It was not my father, but Hylotz. I shouted at him over the howling winds, asking him what the hell this was all about. He just winked and pointed up. A shot rang through the air, and he fell over the cliff.

A familiar fear waved over me. I trembled as I had to catch myself from falling. As I looked up, the storm clouds returned. They surrounded me once again. The cold froze my body.

PART FOUR
MARZANNA
WITH: MYLES

I

Days.

It felt like goddamn days since I'd had a smoke. That crazy black weed we had smoked was intense, but it doubled my craving.

Yet here we are in this godforsaken ship, float'n around the universe look'n for some crazy old homeless man, for what? So we'll all just perish in an intergalactic storm? And yet here we are. Parked right in a flip'n snowbank. Freeze'n our asses off.

What led us here? Cabell's aspirations of saving Earth? Bailey's wish to escape the mundanity of urban life? Maya's chasing her own reflection? I pulled my foot out of the Ondas ocean water which had pooled at the bottom of the ship. No matter how we got here, it was a frig'n disaster. And I could really use a goddamn smoke right about now.

"Where the hell are we?" Fathom said, looking out the window of the ship.

"Your guess is as good as mine," Cabell answered.

"Ain't nothin but blowing snow out there," I said. "Looks rough. Y'know, we *could* be back on Earth. Looks about the same as when we left it."

"I hope so. Last Bastion's bathroom would be heaven right about now."

"There's only one way to find out," said Fathom, reaching to open the door. "It's not budging."

"We're in a goddamn snowbank, that's why." I nearly spat my words out. "This is a frig'n disaster." We tried our doors to no avail. What a waste of time. "Well what's the plan now?" I dared someone to step up and pierce through this shitstorm we'd got ourselves stuck in.

"Rock the ship! Maybe we can rock our way out of it," said Fathom.

Fair enough. Decent point. We started rock'n to and fro, working with staggered momentum. It was minimally effective. Mostly pointless.

"Right. Pretty much an exercise in futility. Never hurts to perform one of those though, eh Cabell?"

Cabell was about to respond before he was interrupted by a roar outside the ship.

"Jesus, Cabell, I know it's been a while since we had a good meal, but you really gotta get a handle on that stomach," I said.

"Shut up Myles. What the hell is out there?"

"Not sure I want to know," Fathom said.

"We may be proper screwed this time, for real," I said.

The ship shifted hard to the right, not through any action of our own. Must have been a goddamn beast outside.

"This ain't good. Not good at all," I said.

Light from the window was eclipsed by a figure with

teeth gnawing into the glass.

"That's a lot of nope for me," I said.

"Look, let's just calm down and wait it out," Cabell said.

"Brilliant idea. Keep doin' what we're doin'. That's why they pay you the big bucks."

Cabell frowned, but didn't respond. He was more generally irritated than specifically angry at me. And to be fair, I wasn't really pissed at him as much as the situation.

We must'a spent hours in that goddamn ship, just wait'n. To be rescued? Naw, probably not. It reminded me of the road trips I took with the old man as a child. What a beast he was, constantly either on the booze, hook'n up with some woman or revel'n in the beauty of nature. But sit'n in this goddamn ship goin' nowhere brings back those memories now. In some ways he was a monster of a man, but hell, he got shit done. And, God bless him, he did show me how to deal with shit in life. Least postmodern urban life where drugs are available 24/7. Jesus, I need a smoke.

✦

I woke up to a biting cold, howl'n wind, icicles form'n under my nose. Christ, I was out in the goddamn snow. How th'hell did this happen? I must'a fell asleep. The others were nowhere around.

I rose to my knees, my face freezing. Snow everywhere; I couldn't see a damn thing. I was shivering, and dizzy. I tried to get to my feet, but the wind wrestled me down to my knees again. This storm was going to be the death of me.

In the confusion of the storm I fell flat on the ground. Again, I tried to stand up, to no avail. I edged forward on my knees, and damn, it wasn't easy, let me tell you.

In my disorientation, I landed on my back once more. I forced myself up with all my might, and I was on my feet and out of the storm. It happened so fast it was surreal. Was I just imagining this, or was I fly'n all over the place?

It was quiet, like I was in the eye of the storm, the snowflakes were swirl'n all around me. Then I saw it. Sweet Jesus. Two antlers in front of me, protude'n into my field of vision. And a vicious face. Teeth barred around a horrible roar!

In my mind, I was running away as fast as possible, but I didn't feel my muscles move. Through the dizziness I realized that I was back in the storm. It was the most bizarre feeling. I'd just witnessed some sort of horrible beast, and somehow got myself out of it, even though I didn't—

The roar came from behind me, and the sound of footfalls. It was chase'n me! I had to get out of there quick, but my body was stiff as a rock. I moved through the storm as best as I could; the beast's howling faded. Somehow, I was moving without even exerting myself. Strange as hell.

This dance continued for quite a while. I moved farther and farther from that horrible beast, until its howls became indistinguishable from those of the wind. It felt like the winds of the storm were picking me up and whisking me along. The cold was horrible. I wondered how my body could withstand so much damn cold without completely shut'n down.

I kept moving, vision blurred. And soon enough I found myself in a dark space. I fell to my knees. Damp, cold, flat, rock. Definitely rock. I was in a cave. And I was happy enough with it. I curled into a ball and, despite the best documentation on survive'n hypothermia, I fell asleep.

II

Through the hazy blur of sleep, I'd entered a dream-like state. I explored a village that appeared from the darkness. It was the same bustling village I'd seen while navigating the ship. It was full of lively youth, rich farmland and a government unified with its people to create a future full of young happy lives.

At first, the winters were not long. But after a few years, they got longer and the snow soon permeated all year round.

The shops stayed open fewer hours in the evening. The kids returned home from playing earlier and earlier. And the people began to get mad at the government for doing nothing.

Even still there was a notion—not only with the government, but with the others—that it would all go away. Surely, obviously, it's only temporary. Seasons change; it doesn't last forever. The day would come when it would all just turn out to be a bad dream, and the kids would play later once again.

But one year, when summer came, the snow did not cease, and the white spiral storms began to grow worse. It didn't help that, during that year there was a great food shortage. The people were angry at the government, insisting something be done. And the government turned to the people and said "It's not our fault. We're doing everything we can." But were they?

In this same year, the town was afflicted with a herd of

moose, apparently looking for food and shelter from the storm. Rumors said that the herd was accompanied by a bearded man perusing the shops with the moose, long after they were closed.

It was not until one day that a shop was broken into, that the government took a stand, its leader with his dark-rimmed glasses suggesting "the bearded man is to blame for this theft. We will find him, and we will imprison him. If any moose are found roaming the city, given the food shortage, it is acceptable to shoot them."

🗡

I woke from the dream, the cave was dark as hell, and I felt like absolute shit. I was starved for food and a smoke. If that beast had been in here, I would've torn its throat out and made a meal of it. 'Course that was a bit ambitious, nonetheless I knew I needed to find the others.

Was this Earth? It was possible, but the storm seemed worse than we'd left it. Visibility outside was near zero and it felt even colder than I've ever known Earth to be.

I edged my way through the darkness, finally finding a doorway. I made my way out into a narrow space and continued onward. To my relief, I saw a light in the distance. When I reached it, I realized it was a candle. So there was some sort of civilization here. Thank God.

I continued down the hall, and found another candle, then another. I followed candles until I found some stairs leading up.

I walked up several floors before finally reaching a wooden door, a candle on either side. I pushed it open slowly. It was a big room with light beaming down from a ceil'n that opened into the sky which was void of the storm. In the middle there were long, broad wooden cases of a greyish-white plant. I brought it close to my face, but it did not exude any smell; the leaves were shaped like stars. It looked a little like the Atavika 'lief. Was this a greenhouse for them?

I walked down another hallway to a wooden door. The door flew out with a gust; The howling wind pushed the door back and forth on its hinges. I could feel the familiar bitter cold of the storm pushing up against me, breaking my skin out into bigger and bigger goosebumps.

Outside, the edge dropped off into a dangerous cliff. I paused for a moment to consider my options. There must be some sort of civilization nearby, and I was starved. I needed to move on—find those people. There was no other reasonable option at this point.

I carefully edged along the cliff not know'n how far down the drop might be but expecting the worst. There was a roar in the distance that made my blood run cold. Goddamn beasts again.

I shivered, considered turning back to regroup. It was too dangerous. Before I could make any progress, there was another howl close by. Out of the snow came the same horrid beast from before, on the path I'd come from, blocking my way.

I backed away from it, but the beast closed in on me fast. I realized now that I'd reached another edge. There was a wooden bridge, but it was derelict; impassable. I edged my way on to it until I reached the part that had fallen apart. The beast roared from the cliffside. I was screwed.

The only escape was to jump to the other side. With

a deep breath, I made a valiant attempt jump across the gap, but I was short. My fingers scraped across the frail wood, but I couldn't get a grip in the snow. At the last second, my hands grabbed a hold of a piece of wood on the other side. I had almost exhaled a relieved sigh when the wood shattered into pieces. I fell, but managed to grip hard onto the dangling rope. The damage was too much and the bridge snapped behind me. I fell, the rope I still clung too swung me forward and I slapped against the other side of the cliff. My grip was loosening. There was no way I could climb up. I held on as long as I could, but it was only a matter of time.

I felt fear rise inside me. If this was really the end, what was the point of it all? My whole life I'd followed in the footsteps of my father, using drugs to ease the pain, to escape from mundanity of life but also, in a way, to avoid having to face the reality that someday, it would all be ultimately lost in an unavoidable fate. Emotions that had lay dormant for years welled up inside me.

I almost gave up when a voice called to me from somewhere out in the storm.

"Do not be afraid, Aaron Myles. Feel the pathway forward through the storm, only when you are at peace, will you feel yourself rise above."

III

The voice seemed to come from above, and I didn't hear it as much as I *felt* it. I made peace with my fate, and I let go. I had lived as well as I could, I had pursued my own happiness and that of others, and I had tried to do the best for everyone. I had a hell of a lot of good times.

"Allow yourself to let go and rise with us. You can rise above by succumbing to your fallible nature."

Through my acceptance of death, I realized a way forward was beyond the physical nature of this world. I allowed myself to let go, but I focused on following the voice.

Then I fell…into nothing. Instead, I rose to the edge of the cliff. A hand grabbed my arm and pulled me in a doorway. The door closed and people lifted me up a stairway. My vision was blurry. I was barely able to move.

We entered a greenhouse like the one I'd found. Through the light I could make out the people that had helped me up here. Long white hair draped from the hoods of their dark cloaks, they looked like some sort of cult.

A woman approached me. She was young and beautiful with close-set eyes, a pale complexion, and bright white irises. "Aaron Myles. So nice for you to join us. We were just musing on how dreadfully lonely it is, living in a derelict castle on a dying planet amid a universal apocalypse. Marcus, please prepare a 'lief for our guest, he's awfully cold."

I struggled to sit upright, my eyes squint'n to make sense of the situation. A bearded man had taken one of the plants from the garden and was wrapping it in a small piece of paper. He sparked a fire with a fire striker and brought it to the paper, a motion that immediately cleared my blurry vision and it brought a great warmth to my heart. I longingly reached out for the spliff.

I felt it warm my entire body as I inhaled it, the warmth seemed to cast the room in a new light. The group of men and women became kindred; I felt as though I could see beyond their hardened features to their youthful essence. What's more, I felt I could nearly *see* their essence as humans. I felt almost like a child again. And the cold didn't bother me one bit. I'd acclimated to it.

"There you go," the woman said. "You're feeling much better now, aren't you?"

"Yes. Yes I am. Thank you.".

"This drug will keep you adjusted through the storm. To be completely honest, we're surprised you made it this far. Unaided humans can't survive a Level 4 storm more than an hour. We had you on radar less than an hour ago, hence our trip to find you."

"Where...am I?"

"Oh, apologies. I should have introduced myself. My name is Nivea and this is the planet of Marzanna. We're delighted to have you, although we're quite confused as to how your ship got you here, given that intergalactic space travel has yet to have been discovered by humans, to our knowledge. Ourselves, we have not even had the opportunity to engage in interstellar travel, and sadly our days are becoming numbered."

I inhaled another puff of the spliff. It was amazing. I was so relaxed, and more attuned to the others and the ambience of the cave. I felt so warm.

"I'm glad I found you," I told them. "But what about my friends? There are some nasty beasts out there—"

"Ah, the Bies. Yes, they have become a serious nuisance since their mutation. They will attack immediately, and we can not communicate with them. If it wasn't for our fortress, we'd be dead.

"Don't worry about your friends. We already have a search party looking for them. They will be fine. Now, lets head back to the castle and get you some food. You look like you've been shaken by the storm for way too long."

"I won't argue with you," I said.

I stood and found that the drug had dulled the pain from before. We made our way up through the greenhouse and out yet another door. At the edge of the cliff, there was an incredible view. The storm stretched out like a sea of mist, leading a long path to mountains in the distance. At the top of the mountain, there was a castle, beautifully resting high in the air above the encroaching storm.

"Now, Aaron Myles, given your temperament and vulnerabilities getting here, I believe it's quite evident that you are at best novice to the teleportative potential of the storm."

"The what?"

"Well, remember when I *spoke* to you when you nearly fell off that bridge?"

"Yes."

"Well, then, how did you survive?"

"I fell and I just…well, I just landed at the other end?"

"Right. You landed *up* at the other end of the bridge. In short, you *rode* through the storm. A Level 4 storm has teleportative capabilities. You can *ride* the storm for short distances. Eventually it will peter out, but it will last for a good five minutes or so, if you're good at it, and if you have assistance from the 'lief."

"You're not saying that…"

"Yes. That's exactly what I'm saying. We have to *ride*

across the cloud to the castle. It's the only way. The divide acts as the castle's moat, keeping the Bies, and—at one time—unwelcome villagers away."

"You can't be serious. There's no way I can do that. I barely made it here alive, somehow, but I can't cross a massive distance like that in five minutes."

Nivea took my face in her hands and gazed into my eyes. Quite intimidating, considering her beauty. Through her eyes, she spoke, but not through speech.

"You can, and you will. How did you get here? How did you escape the Bies? There's no way you would have made it this far without leveraging the power of the storm to guide you through. We've watched you from when you first left the ship. You've traversed a great distance to get here. And how did you do this? By giving up? No. Risk exists in all ventures. The only antidote for fear is action in the face of adversity. We must constantly be throwing ourselves into the storm and growing to meet the dreams of ourselves along the way."

"Alright. I will try, but can you help me?"

"Of course," she said. *"Hold my hand and stay present with me. As long as you feel me close beside you, you will not fall. And the others, you can feel them too can't you? They will be all around us. Stay with us, and we will cross the storm."*

I let my fear wash away, like I did when I let go from the bridge. Holding Nivea's hand, we both fell into the storm.

IV

Through some unseen magic, I was surfing through the storm, and I felt a presence with me. I was again impressed with the vision of the village, but this time the view followed the man with dark-rimmed glasses. He traversed across a winter forest with a team of hunters, rifles strung over their backs, intent on finding something, or—someone.

Their journey came to an end as they hid in a cave and spied on an older man with a beard who was walking along the cliff-side. He turned to face them, and with a shot, he fell over the side of the cliff.

Riding the storm turned out easier than I thought, 'course the drug they gave me was work'n wonders. My body felt cool, yet I felt warm inside. It was like I'd acclimated to the storm.

We came to another cliff's edge and worked our way along a cliffside and into a cave. This led to the foot of a gray castle that was intermittently cloaked by the mist of the white death storm and covered in the 'liefs I'd seen earlier. It was truly breathtaking.

The castle looked like something right out of Earth's medieval period, suggesting their civilization was less advanced. Though with Nivea's apparent clairvoyance, it seemed like they were considerably more advanced for their time. I wanted the answers to this, but was content to just take it all in, revelling in the drug's effect.

The gatehouse opened for us, and we passed through a beautiful stone court. We traversed a vegetable garden and entered a threshold into to the castle keep. We ascended a long spiral staircase, and the walls were covered with a viny plant that looked a lot like the 'liefs from before. At the top of the stairs, we moved into an open room that overlooked a vast sea of the foggy, white mist of the storm. Another planet loomed on the horizon. In the middle of the room there was a stone column, with flat surface and plates of food laid out for us. The thought occurred to me…had Nivea telepathically alerted of our presence?

Nonetheless, I quickly stuffed my face with the delicious vegetables and fruits provided, revelling in the first decent meal I'd had since this whole thing started. When I was finished, my eyes met Nivea's who was eyeing me inquisitively. Maybe she couldn't read all my thoughts and was trying to pry further beyond her capabilities.

"Thank you for the meal," I said.

"You're quite welcome, Aaron Myles."

"Look, I have a ton of questions, right, but the one foremost in my mind is, why so nice? Why are you treating me so well when you have no idea where I've come from?"

She laughed.

"Oh my, Mr. Myles, we have more knowledge of your origins than you expect. However, there is still more we'd like to know about what brought you here. Never mind that. Right now, your comfort is of our utmost priority. We want you to know that you can stay here as long as you want, and you're entirely safe. You can have as much food as you want, and your friends are welcome also. We have made contact with them now and are bringing them back to the castle."

"How do you know so much?"

"We are an old people, despite our appearance. Our planet has undergone a lot of political struggles leading us to an extended—medieval period, as your planet would say—but it's nothing we can't overcome through patience and compassion. Yet no struggle has been so poignant, so *enlightening*, as this white death storm." She cleared her throat, her brilliant smile gleamed as the gentle mist of the storm brushed along her cheeks.

"Our people—my ancestors—veered away from the medieval dynasties in rebellion against an oppressive regime, physically removing themselves from castles like these and retreating to villages where a democratic form of government lived on for ages unaffected by the withering regal class.

"Yet in my day, unwittingly, our democracy would elect a potential tyrant, William Duncan, a man who—while initially a strong, powerful and compassionate leader—would eventually lead us into ruin in wake of the death storm.

"To be fair, a lot of it was out of his hands. Any government coming up against an environmental catastrophe of this magnitude would be in over its head, but Duncan internalized it, and—perhaps through anger or some form of vengeance—found a scapegoat in the trickling groups of Bies that had sought food and shelter in our villages."

"Despite blowback from the majority of our people, Duncan enacted legislation which permitted slaying of the beasts, and a volatile right-wing minority group took this as carte blanche to initiate some of the worst conditions we've seen for animals in our history.

"As an admitted 'radical' left faction, we accepted defeat and mobilized from villages at a time when the death storm was ramping up to full force and the chances of survival outside the villages was dire at best. Yet we found salvation against the storm in the form of a drug: the Marzanna 'lief.

"The drug had several beneficial side effects when paired with the storm, the least of which being what you'd refer to on your planet as 'hallucination.' As we investigated further, we found these visions were more real than we first assumed. It became evident that this drug was a gateway. Not only to our own minds, but to the many others stretching beyond our planet, reaching far, far into the various worlds of the universe."

While Nivea spoke, the cylindrical column next to us slowly opened, revealing the white dusty air of the storm, which spilled out into the room.

"Beyond this—and of more immediate benefit—the 'lief had a property that allowed our bodies to survive for much longer periods within the storm. And that was just what we needed to sustain a liveable life outside the villages in—ironically enough—our former medieval homes.

"That is how the Breaus formed. We are a small people that have outlived most of our planet that has died in the storm."

Nivea paused, allowing me to take it all in. It was beginning to make sense.

"What happened to the village?" I said.

"The village is no more. The people there did not survive the death storm; they looked on us as treasonous and rejected us outright. They foolishly died in their own ignorance, despite our attempts to help."

"But Earth…" I said, "…how do you know so much about Earth?"

"In short, the storm. You see this column which allows for the channel of storm air? Well, when paired with Marzanna 'lief, *this* is what we use to learn about the universe. There are many others out there that don't respond, but many that do. They have recognized their own potential for communication through the storm."

"Planets like yours—Earth—have not yet recognized us as valid. Those that have responded to us have provided great information, but when they've gone to their leaders, friends, and family they've been, at worst, looked upon as insane. We have seen people confined to psychiatric institutions.

"Yet, we haven't given up hope. As Breaus, we remain focused and dedicated to reaching out and discovering worlds through the storm. We relish the information we uncover in the universe as paramount to our ability to someday survive the storm."

I stared at the column of storm air. If everything Nivea said was true, then the universe really must be a big place.

"Indeed, it is," Nivea said, reading my thoughts. "Incredibly so. And you're about to see just how big it is."

The wooden door opened to reveal another Breau bringing the graying Marzanna 'liefs on a platter, along with a fire striker, cloth and flint. The Breau took our food plates and left the room. Nivea began the process of rolling the leaves into the flint. My eyes watered in anticipation. Voices—other Breaus—could be heard echoing in the castle hallways.

I became hypervigilant to the sights sounds of the sounds around the castle in anticipation of smoking the 'lief. For the first time in my life, I felt part of something big. Like I was witnessing true magic, something that could really change the world.

A blaze of light and heat exploded into the air as Nivea hit the fire striker and lit the joint. She held it out to me, and I took several puffs. The warmth began to fill my body.

"Now Aaron Myles, I know you're excited for this," she said, taking my hand in hers, "but please remain grounded. I'll be here to help you through this, but you're about to experience something relatively few have, and perhaps few will. You must remain grounded; it is important not to let go completely. Although sometimes that may be tempting, we can't let you go."

I nodded. My eyes must have been growing feverishly wide in anticipation of the sensation.

"Now," she spoke to me through the storm, *"please lie back. Feel your head cool gently against the airstream of the storm. Close your eyes. Breath deeply with me. You can hear me. The sounds of the castle will start to…drift, let…body… recede…"*

…distance, time, temperature, constructs, all constructs, floating far above Marzanna, through space, so many avenues, so many directions. Each action could lead a different way. Each road bears fruits to another world…

…Earth…somewhere, it is visible, still ticking along ravished with the storm. My family, further back in time, my father, I can feel him with me, somehow, my presence exists with him, all those adventurous trips into the wilderness, magic just like this, some kind of otherworldly dial leading in every imaginable direction…

…There are many Earths…many different versions, each with slight variations, the universe is so large. Look, there, is a

planet like a flower in a multifaceted garden with a wild jungle where we met Maya and there are millions of different versions of it like reflections in a mirror…

…And Ondas where Onesia saved us, and other planets varying in habitability, vibrance and life, what other worlds exist out there? It's beautiful…

…And minds too, like this small planet Aquila with creatures defending against the storm foolishly with metal barriers…"they are protecting from the storm, my king," says a wild-eyed, short elvish girl with fire and passion in her eyes for her ruler with a face of great concern for his people—I can feel their thoughts as if my own, as if I am them…but they will die at the hand of the storm, I can see that is a highly likely outcome…

…And Marzanna, I can see now, it is a planet much like Earth, but it has been destroyed by the storm. The storm is at nearly its highest intensity, many lives have been lost…

…And the Bies…I can hear them, I can hear their anger, their hatred of humanity, their disgust and their "kill them all! Kill the humans! They killed our loved ones! Destroy them completely! They must face the same fate they thrust on us for the storm! All except the bearded man! They must die!"

…But the 'bearded man'…what about this? Nivea? He was a friend to the Bies, yes. I can see in their minds. He helped them through the storm. He— ("the effect wears off from one area if you stay too long," Nivea tells me)—he is…Hylotz. Terral B. Hylotz…Yes, Nivea, he was welcomed here by the Breaus during their crucial time…he was compassionate with the Bies and helped them live…he was celebrated as a Breau and— ("the poignant effect only lasts so long,")—he was celebrated…before… he— ("the effect is disappearing…")

V

I sat up, my mind racing.

"Take a deep breath," Nivea said. "You will get over it."

"I've got so many questions," I said, panting deeply. "Hylotz, the bearded man. He...we saw him too. That is how we received the ship..."

"Terral, Breau Hylotz," Nivea said. "Yes, he was with us. He was the one who encouraged smoking the Marzanna 'lief. He was crucial to our survival. We have the highest regard for him before he...disappeared. Are you saying he is associated with this...ship?"

"Yes," I said.

Nivea paused, thinking. I could hear her thoughts echoing in my mind: *"he spoke of a ship, his mind was vivid with images of other worlds, could he have been literally travelling to them all this time?"*

"Yes," I said. "It must be!"

"This ship...we need to find it."

"Yes."

"No, Aaron Myles. Do you realize, how incredible this discovery is? However it's possible that this ship exists, it's now an essential part of our continued survival, and would be indispensable to our growth in the universe!"

"Yes," I shouted, standing up and walking around. The door opened to reveal Fathom and Cabell.

"Fathom! Cabell!" I cried in excitement. I ran up and hugged them both. "Marzanna 'lief, it's fascinating. The universe is massive, there is hope for saving Earth, and it looks like Terral Hylotz has been whirling around the universe and smoking up in the ship!"

They stared at me blankly.

"Don't you see? It's this 'lief! It lets you see beyond the limits of your perspective. You can unite with the minds of others in planets far away. Just like the ship has taken us here, somehow this 'lief can do the same thing with our minds."

"Aaron Myles, you should calm down," Nivea said. "Maybe we gave you too much of the 'lief."

"No, you don't understand. I'm virtually indestructible with this." I took a spliff lying on the outstanding platter and inhaled a huge puff before Nivea took it from me.

"Myles," she said.

"No, It's Okay. It's powerful, so poignant, I can see through the storm. I can see beyond the confines of these walls. Even now, I can see many Earths, many worlds, like ours, which thrive, and maybe someday we can meet them. And this 'lief, it *protects* from the storm. Don't you see! It will allow you to *exist* through the storm."

"Yes Myles," Cabell said, "We know that, but…"

"No, You don't. You see, I can actually *ride* the storm." I ran over to the ledge of the castle despite the yelling of the others. I suddenly felt I understood my father. He'd always been so much freer than I, ready for adventure at any whim. I'd always been the one to hold back. The truth is that no number of drugs could bring back the exhilarating rush of taking the world on, facing life instead of trying to stay safe along the sidelines.

There was something more to this feeling than the others knew, something much bigger, and maybe, somehow,

I could make them see. I stood on the ledge despite their screams. They ran to me but, too late. I let myself fall back, like a scuba diver into the sea of storm clouds below.

Foolishly, they would cry as the Breaus stated, "he is no longer with us."

They'd return to the ship, but not without the valuable knowledge they now had: the Marzanna 'lief would allow its smoker to transcend the storm and survive within it for longer periods of time.

In a short time, they came to realize the ship operated in a similar way to transcendence, taking the pilot to destinations of his or her deep desires.

They learned more of the war between the Bies and the village that slaughtered them. They learned how Hylotz and the Bies were to blame for stealing food, and how Duncan had waged a war on the Bies who had mutated into vicious killing machines.

Could the Bies be quelled? The question was raised, and Fathom declared he was beginning to be able to communicate with them, although they were not receptive.

Yet Fathom was insistent that he could reach them, if only he could travel to Kostroma, moon of Marzanna. He was insistent that the Bies must be quelled, that is, after all, what we're all here for; the prolonged continuation of the many; the chance for something better for everyone.

They'd find the ship, surviving the mutated Bies, and they'd continue the journey, hopefully saving the Bies and travelling across the storm, with Fathom piloting, to... Kostroma.

FATHOM PILOTS

As the coldness melted away, my body became wet. I shivered. There was a crack, and then ice that surrounded me broke into a flood of water that splashed onto the floor. I gasped for air.

Nearby, a similar splash could be heard, and a woman with a clipboard dressed in a white nurse outfit walked up next to me, her brown hair drenched in water, her brow furrowed, her dark brown eyes were displeased with me.

"You?" she spat.

"I? uh..."

She sighed. "Alright, lets head down to the morgue, if we must."

The room was full of file cabinets for keeping medical records. She opened a door and led the way down a long staircase. It must have gone on for a good fifteen minutes, before she opened another door to a dark room lit by a shoddy florescent flicker. The far wall had cases built into the wall. They were for keeping corpses.

"I'm surprised you're even still around," she said. "I guess we need all the help we can get, these days."

I shrugged.

"We need you to finish up as quickly as possible. I know this is your first time, but there will be many more bodies soon enough."

"More bodies?"

"Shhh," she said, placing her index finger over my mouth. "Just get to work. The subject was mutilated, torn limb to limb by some awful beast. Just clean up the mess, okay? Do you think you can handle that?" She pointed at the wall where one of the cases was pulled out, revealing a sheet over a corpse. I gasped.

"What is going on here?" I said, turning back towards the nurse, but she was gone. The door we'd come from was closed. I jiggled the knob. Locked.

I walked over to the corpse. The sheet completely covered the body. There was a mop resting in the corner of the wall. It hit me. Was this Myles? A shiver ran through me.

I knew what I had to do. I had to remove the sheet. I took a deep breath and pulled it down and…nothing. There was nothing there, but an eerie chill rose through the room.

The cold grew and grew, and the brick walls began to crack. Slowly at first, then much faster, big chunks of brick were falling apart, and the cold was unbearable. The ceiling began to fall apart, and the walls and—I had to jump onto the gurney which was the only solid item left. I pulled the sheet over me, shivering, covering my entire head.

When the cold finally eased off a little, I pulled the sheet down just enough to peak outside. There was no gurney now. I was hovering in darkness. Stars were above, below, and all around. I was in space. A vacuum was pulling me in many directions, yet I remained intact. The sheet had dissipated.

"Thank goodness you're still here," a man said from behind

me. I turned around to see he was bald, in a white lab coat. He also had a clipboard and was staring at me. "We had doubts you'd make it this far, but your talents now can be exercised. You still have a long way to go."

"My talents?"

"Yes. Many lives are at stake. Many are counting on you to step up and help end the suffering." The man pointed behind me. Again, I turned around. Behind me, there were moose, rabbits and many other animals staring expectantly.

I turned back to the man, but he had changed. He had a beard. He was Hylotz. Still in a lab coat.

"What's this all about?" I demanded.

"It's too cold," Hylotz said, with a smile. He raised a joint to his lips and took a puff. "Too cold to tell how it'll turn out. Help them. They will help you."

He took another puff, then handed me his joint. In the spirit of the moment, I shrugged and took a puff. As the warmth glowed inside me. That familiar peace returned.

"You'll be pulled in many directions," Hylotz said. "Help them all. Someday…" his voice trailed off. The storm was approaching from far off in space. It was encircling from all sides, closing in, and Hylotz had faded away. I braced myself as the coldness grew once again.

KOSTROMA
WITH: FATHOM

We gently landed in the snow, a puff of which flew up over the windshield temporarily obstructing our view. Not that it would matter; the storm was raging on just as bad as on Marzanna.

My mind was in disarray with the events of the last hour. Seeing Myles jump was traumatic. On Earth, you'd spend hours of counselling and mental health treatment, and the post-traumatic stress would last for decades. This wasn't Earth.

"I don't know about this," I said.

"The tragedy we've faced from the Bies has been horrible," Nivea said. "We've lost many Breaus to these beasts. If there is any chance you can stop them, Jacob Fathom, we need you to try."

Nivea opened a brown sack she had taken with her and pulled out the spliffs, one for each of us. She struck a fire and lit them. We each took one.

"And what if it doesn't work? What then?" Cabell looked concerned.

"It will work. If it doesn't, we've got the ship. We can try to find another solution.

"Very well," I lit the joint and inhaled. The warmth flowed through my body and I began to hear the echoes of voices in the distance—the Bies—revelling in anger and disdain for humanity.

"They hate us," I said.

"Yes but, can you talk to them?" said Nivea.

"I...can't. They are too far away. My voice would just be an after-thought to them.

"Then you'll have to go out," said Nivea.

"You can't be serious."

"What other options do we have? Stay at a distance from them but try to reach one. We'll come with you."

"This is incredibly dangerous," said Cabell.

"We have to try," I said with a shrug.

We opened the doors to the ship and slowly made our way out into the storm. Upon entering the strong, powdery snow, the Bies' thoughts became amplified tenfold.

"The humans are here. I can smell them."

"They're coming to kill us."

"Stop them!"

I turned to retreat to the ship.

"Wait," Nivea said. "Try to reach them."

I paused and called out through the storm to them. *"We come in peace. We just want to help."*

"Anything?" Nivea asked.

I was silent for a moment, then the responses came.

"How can you help, foolish human. You caused this disaster, you killed many of us. You caused our anger!"

"We did not cause it. We are against it," I thought. *"The people who caused it are no longer with us. We seek only peace. We want to help you survive the storm."*

"You are the cause of it! How could you help?"

Suddenly a movement came from my left, a beast jumped from the snow and attacked, biting my leg and causing me to scream out in pain. I fell to the ground. Nivea and Cabell kneeled to my side, but we were surrounded by Bies ready to attack."

"No," I screamed, through thought. *"We mean to help. We are suffering from the storm like you. We can help!"*

"You are the storm. You are the anger. And now you will die as a result like you have done to all our brothers and sisters!"

The pain was immense. I knew I would pass out soon from lack of blood.

"We are vulnerable to you now. You can kill us. Just know that we know of the bearded man, Hylotz, we know that he helped you. He was human like us. He helped you live through the storm. Do you remember him?"

Silence.

"He helped you, and we seek to help you too. We know how to help you survive the storm; we want to give you a solution."

Reading their minds, I could feel them remembering their history, the history of Kostroma before the storm came, when they were once a great race living in a warm climate. The planet had been full of life, before the storm came and a bridge connected both Kostroma and Marzanna, exposing them to the village that massacred them.

"We know of the tragedy of the village; the people of the village are all dead now. We are against their violence and always have been. We have a way to deal with the storm. Maybe someday Kostroma can be the world it once was, and you can survive to see it."

I grabbed the brown sack from Nivea and opened it

for the Bies. They roared a horrible roar and in a dying pain and fear, I lost consciousness.

"Hey man, sorry about that whole plan to kill you thing. We greatly appreciate your offering."

I opened my eyes to find I was in the ship. Nivea and Cabell had tied a cloth around my leg, and I was stable.

"It's just that, you can't really expect to massacre so many of us without consequences, right? Anyway man, you dudes are alright. Like really alright. And this plant, this, what do you call it? 'lief? This is the shit, for real man. Some real good stuff. We haven't tasted anything this good since the bearded man was around, the 'Hylotz' dude you speak of. Capital guy, best of kinds. Absolute legend, himself."

"We gave them the Marzanna 'lief and lit it for them," said Cabell. "They seem to like it."

"They certainly do," I said. "They are quite mellow."

"Look man, you guys are cool. We will pass on word of you to our brothers and sisters. You want us to lay off the vicious-ness, just keep producing this shit and we shouldn't have any problem convincing the others."

"What are they saying?" Nivea asked.

"They want us to manufacture Marzanna 'lief for them."

"Well that's definitely doable," she replied. "I can reach out to the Breaus through the storm. We can make it happen."

"We can make that happen," I said to the Bies. *"Absolutely."*

"Right on. We'll go now and let you get on about your busi-

ness. Please prepare more of this stuff as soon as possible. Best of luck on your travels."

"*Thanks,*" I said to them.

"Well, I think that actually worked," I said.

"Yes," Nivea said. "This ship is already working wonders."

"This is great," Cabell said. "But is there any way we can actually return to Earth? This 'lief could be really helpful to humans."

"Well, we can try to do that," Nivea said. "But the ship, despite its amazing power, doesn't appear to be a perfect science. We're lucky it even brought us here, to Kostroma. How did you make this happen, Fathom?"

"Like you said, Nivea. How you focus through the storm when you reach through it: with intention. And, to be honest, the drugs seemed to help. I focused my mind on Kostroma, but beyond that, I just felt the utmost need to help. Like, strongly, just like Terral Hylotz, I wanted to help the Bies. I didn't want them to continue to suffer the fate that had befallen them, I didn't want them to die in the storm, and I didn't want them to kill others. And like Myles said, in a way, I wished for this with my all. All of my emotions, all of my thoughts, all were centered around this one goal."

"Well," said Nivea, "maybe we could try to reach out to my friends in Aras as well. They are quite far away in the universe, but they are the strongest most advanced civilization we know of. They have lots of ideas that haven been effective for helping to mitigate the damage of the death storm, and they sure could provide some suggestions for Earth. While they have left their planet, they have not been able to navigate beyond their galaxy. Meeting them would be a positive step for the Universal Storm Alliance, and we could really take great strides towards ending this storm for good. I'd really like to pilot. I'd like to try to reach Aras."

"Well, lets go," I said.

Nivea took the wheel and the ship lifted off the snowy surface of Kostroma, bringing us on a new journey.

NIVEA PILOTS

I swam through a surreal universe, through space, in search of Saranyu. The storm began to fade, as did space, and I was left sitting on a rocky mountainside. Above, ships fought shooting lasers and missiles with ferocious accuracy. Mechanical robots attacked each other on rocky terrain that continued into the distance and met another planet on the horizon. A small moon was visible in space.

In front of me there was a fallen robot. I could feel Saranyu's presence, but I could not see her. An orb of light gently fell from the storm above. When it reached the ground, it expanded into vision of my old friend. His beard had grayed more with the storm. Terral Breau Hylotz.

"Nivea, some day you may help stop suffering of our world," he says. "But the path will be long and fraught with conflict, with many minds to sway. Remember to never give up on your friends. There is one race that is very dangerous — "

I wish I could have continued to hear him, but his voice trailed off as the storm swept in returning the familiar cold.

ARAS
WITH: NIVEA

I

The ship spun like a whirlwind as I wrestled to regain control. After a few spins, I adjusted. We exited the storm, and I was struck immediately by the beauty of the sunrise. A blazing pink sun partnered by two smaller moons brightened the sky, painting a beautiful landscape that some cultures might suggest was akin to divine.

Steadying the wheel remained a challenge. It was shaking beyond control.

We traversed a deep blue mountainous terrain with bright red vegetation that I recalled from my storm talks with Saranyu. The bushes swayed back and forth in waves with the wind. We had made it Aras. So, it was true. The ship really could connect you where you desired.

This thought alone was warming, but I was concerned with our ability to make it to Aras's city, as we were essentially flying blind.

"Look over there," Fathom said, pointing. It was another cloud of the storm spiralling up into space. I realized our potential to reach Saranyu was, quite literally, through the storm clouds.

"I'm going to try to land," I said.

"Be careful not to drive into the storm, it may drive us back across space," Cabell said.

The ship shook as we brought it down on a cliffside, close to the storm.

"Well, that's a great landing," Fathom said. "You're the first of us to not crash the ship. Impressive."

"Thank you," I said. "I've had a lot of mental practice with Saranyu. She has taught me flying techniques through the storm. Let us head to it, maybe we can reach her."

We stepped out onto the blue, alien mountain. The clay-like soil squished against our feet. The red trees swayed in a light wind. A nearby pond glowed pink in reflection of the sky above. We finally reached a summit that touched upon the storm. Fathom opened the box with the Marzanna 'lief and lit it for me. I smoked it, then walked into the storm.

My mind drifted up into space, across the universe, then back to Aras, where I could feel Saranyu's presence.

"Are you there? Saranyu?"

I waited for some time, before her image appeared in front of me.

"I'm here. And you are too, I feel it. You are on Aras?"

"Yes, I'm here, with friends."

"How is it possible?"

"We have a ship. We don't know where it came from, but it lets us travel through the storm."

"We are searching for your location with our systems now. Yes, if you can proceed northwest, you will reach us."

"Great. We will head back to the ship and begin —"

My speech was disconnected by a jolting of my body, I was being pulled from the storm.

"What is happening?" I cried. Fathom looked horrified as he stared up above.

"We've got to get back to the ship." He shouted, as he ran back down the mountainside. "Another ship is shooting at us!"

II

I followed behind Cabell and Fathom, running as fast as I could. We retraced the steps that had brought us here.

"What happened?" I yelled.

"Some ship from above was shooting down at us. It looks like it's landing."

When we finally reached our ship, another ship appeared in front of us, heading directly towards us. It looked identical to our own.

"Get in!" Cabell cried, and as we closed the door laser fire hit us, causing us to sway left and right.

"This is crazy!" I shouted.

"Well, at least we know this ship is durable," Cabell said.

"Nivea, you're the one with the best knowledge of how to fly this thing," said Fathom. "Get us out of here!"

I wrapped my hands around the driving wheel and our ship jumped to life. We lifted off the ground but were now face to face with the ship that had attacked us.

"Look out!" Cabell yelled. As we changed direction, the other ship did as well. Both ships collided, but our attacker was sent it into a downward spiral and crashed into the ground.

"Go, go, go!" Fathom cried.

I brought us back up into the air.

"Fathom do you have a compass?" I asked.

"Yes."

"Get it out. We need to be going northwest."

"Turn to the left," Fathom said. "Just a bit more. Yes, that's it!"

We continued our flight, unhindered by the ship that had attacked us earlier. It wasn't following. We did not come up on anymore instances of the storm.

We flew for a good half hour before purple lights sparkled in our eyes. It was the sun reflecting off glass—the city of Aras. Spaceships wove in and out of great metallic glass buildings, rays of light bouncing off their glass in bright blotches, a flurry of spaceships bustling with their daily business.

I recalled that this would be a busy workday for Aras. They were a highly advanced civilization, highly focused on space exploration. Like many advanced civilizations, they were set on exploring the universe and finding a solution to the death storm. They had already expanded beyond their planet and into their galaxy.

The sky was filled with the roars of spaceships as they blazed through the sky. The sound frightened me more than it would if it were an actual threat.

"Well this certainly is a pleasure, compared to what we've encountered up until now," Cabell said. "Perhaps we could even find a reasonable washroom in this place."

"What the hell is it with you and washrooms, Cabell?" Fathom asked. "Why don't you just go anywhere? That's what we've all been doing."

Cabell shot a frown at Fathom. "Paruresis is no joke, Fathom. Not all of us can just go anywhere. I'm just seek-ing...optimal conditions. And this place looks like it would have something."

"The Aras are highly advanced," I said, "and they have technology that counters the storm. However, it is not an infallible technology, and it is growing wearier as the storm grows in intensity."

We walked along the landing pad and entered an open space which consisted of tall building with ports for ships extending high up and down. An elevator took us up to a new level. We explored the area.

We were on a sidewalk of sorts, with ships flying back and forth along the street, which was essentially just a space between buildings; there was a pinkish haze. People walked beside us, dressed in very plain navy-blue clothes, a type of uniformed wear. There were shops lining the block we were on. The buildings rose high up into the sky.

There was a café with drinks displayed on a sign. We stepped in and made our way to the bar, sitting next to two others speaking in an alien language.

The Aras were a soft-spoken species, their language had an absence of harsher consonants, but there was much more subtlety of expression in facial recognition and body language.

A bartender approached and spoke to us in their alien language. Realizing our inability to understand him, he provided us with three drinks and proceeded to step into the back, speaking on what apparently was an electronic device attached to his ear.

"What is this?" Fathom said, swirling his brownish-yellow drink around in his glass.

"A turbo-brew," I replied. "This is a drink many Aras use to get them through the day. It is a mixture of caffeine, alcohol, and a multivitamin. Some people swear by it to the near complete absence of meals.

"How do you know all this?" Fathom asked.

"I have been in contact with this society for quite a while through the storm. I never thought I'd get to meet them, though, so as you can imagine, this is an immensely moving experience."

"I'm sold," Fathom said, taking a sip of the drink. "Ugh, it's disgusting!"

"Wait a moment," I said, "It's adjusting to your taste buds."

I watched as Fathom's expression turned from disgust to awe. Then, Saranyu appeared. Her narrow eyes welcomed us. Her dusky skin was an expression of her many years as a fighter pilot for Aras Defense, and her dark blue uniform matched her pupils beautifully. She handed us each electronic translator which we attached to our ears.

"It is good to finally meet you, Nivea," she said. We pressed our palms up against each other's and stared diligently into each other's eyes for a moment, a greeting I understood was customary for them.

"And this is your crew of discoverers?" she asked, smiling upon Fathom and Cabell.

"Yes, this is the crew. They are loving the turbo-brew."

"Terrific," she said, laughing.

"One thing I should mention, Saranyu, is that we were attacked by a ship on our way here. We have no idea where it came from. It did not appear to be of Aras."

"That's strange. I've been at Aras Defense Command all day; we didn't see anything on the radar. Well, we'll look into it, but for now, lets head up to my office and discuss this amazing discovery!"

III

The sun flitted through the window and as we road up an elevator. I could see ocean rigs in the distance.

The view of the horizon from Saranyu's office was breathtaking, and the walls were posted with planets and star maps.

"After Nivea advised us of it when you were all still on Marzanna, we have been reaching out to the Universal Storm Alliance, and we're unsure as to where this ship has come from," said Saranyu. "Certainly, it is outside of our galaxy which we have near fully mapped. We don't have the technology to travel beyond our galaxy yet.

"Initially we thought it could be Delexeeaon technology, but we have reached out to them, and they have never heard of such a thing. They are only able to perform smaller galactic stints, like ourselves. So, crew, what do we know about this ship?"

"Not a lot," said Cabell. "It can travel great distances in space, and it has brought us to some pretty crazy places, thus far."

"Do you have any idea where it came from?" asked

Saranyu, walking over to the window to observe the ship from her office. The ship was now protected by Aras security.

"They have no idea," said Nivea. "It appears to have been piloted by Terral Breau Hylotz who, as you know, introduced us to the Marzanna 'lief. If that's the case, there is a whole other layer to this old man that we were not aware of.

"Eventually, the ship ended up on Earth, an alpha classed planet quite far from us, and that's where this crew found it. Terral never mentioned a ship to us."

Saranyu walked over to the window and looked out at the ship. "It's really a beautiful construction," she said, "How does it work?"

"That's another curious thing," said Nivea. "It appears to operate according to the pilot's own inner motivations. It seems to connect to your pulse, and by some alien technology, it appears to be linking the pilot to a uniquely suited location somewhere in the universe. My intention, for example, was to pilot it here, and it seemed to resonate with that intention and brought us here."

Saranyu stood idle, staring at the ship. "If that's true, this ship is powerful beyond our knowledge. Could this mean there is an alien species beyond our level of competence out there?"

"Yes. There must be. With that, maybe there is hope for defeating the death storm."

"This is incredible," Saranyu said. "I must pilot it."

"Certainly," I said. "However, the crew is now trying to return to Earth. We are hoping to make first contact with earth and help them cope with the storm, with the Marzanna 'lief." I pulled a Marzanna 'lief out of my brown bag. I laid one on the table for Saranyu.

"Ah yes, the Marzanna 'lief," Saranyu said. "This will alleviate the struggle Aras has when reaching out across the storm. The drug we use for transcendence has its limitations. It will be most helpful to us. Thank you."

"It's no problem," I said. "Now, lets head down to the ship."

The ship was protected by a small army of Arasans with big laser-guns. Saranyu whispered to a few. There was a congregation of people gathered outside looking upon the ship with the utmost curiosity.

"There's quite a stir about the potential of the ship, but we're keeping its origins under wraps," said Saranyu. "Not for much longer, though. They're about to see what all the fuss is about."

We walked over to the ship and slipped in. A shrill alarm blared through the air. I covered both ears, startled. A green laser blasted right next to me, causing a nearby cargo box to explode.

"Get in the ship," Saranyu yelled.

I jumped in the ship and we looked out through the window to see a fleet of ships, just like our own, soaring through the air.

"Where did they come from?" Fathom cried.

"They're just like the ship that attacked us when we first arrived on Aras," Cabell said.

Another explosion near the ship.

"Aras Defense, come in," said Saranyu. "We've got a whole fleet attacking us!"

We could hear the response from Aras Defense coming through Saranyu's radio. "We see them. We're overwhelmed. No idea where they came from. They are destroying the city. Pilot the ship and get out of here if you can. We'll deal with them. We have our fleet mobilizing."

Saranyu initiated the ship immediately and we were air bound. A ship came up on our tail and we dodged a laser shot.

"I have no idea how to access the weapons, if there even are any," cried Saranyu. "We're going to have to stick to evasion tactics."

Saranyu rolled the ship to avoid another laser shot, but more ships were appearing through the window following us. They seemed fixated on us and our ship. They were not attacking the city and they were right on our tail.

The Aras were shooting at them from below, but they were undeterred. I saw one ship to our right side take a hit, but it glowed a bright green with some sort of force field technology.

"Hold tight," Saranyu yelled, and she dove down between the high skyscrapers of the city, leading us directly into citizen traffic.

We came up on several other citizen ships heading directly for us. She evaded each one, but some of the attacking ships were not as lucky. One smashed head-on into an oncoming citizen ship and they both fell into the ground below.

"Damnit, they're not letting up!" I screamed, as a laser shot flew across the side of my field of vision. This was way more intense than I had ever expected in the stories Saranyu had told me, and I instantly regretted my decision to come to Aras.

Saranyu turned us around a sharp corner, and we came up quick on the glass of a building. I thought we were about to crash into, but we narrowly avoided it and managed to pull away.

"Let's see how fast this thing can go," Saranyu said.

We held on to the side of the ship as we ascended at a nauseating pace. Glancing below, I could not immediately see the ships. I was looking for the storm, but it was not nearby. Then I saw her plan.

She pulled high up into the sky, the pinkish sky gave way to darker hues, and the cabin became colder as we entered space.

There were no ships visible below, but Saranyu kept up the jostling pace. We were going faster than I ever imagined possible. After mere minutes, we were completely free of the planet. The ships did not appear to have followed. They'd dropped completely off our radar.

IV

"Who the hell were they?" said Cabell.

"They're after the ship," Saranyu said. "No doubt in my mind. Looks like there's a price to pay for this asset that's landed in your lap."

"Believe me, we've already paid dearly for this ship. I'd gladly give it to them if it actually returned us to Earth."

"What now?" I asked.

"There's somewhere we can hide out for now. It's a research station behind Aris, Aras's first moon. It's a station where they study the storm. We should be good there for a while, and we can reach out to Aras as my local communicator won't reach them now."

We travelled through space for about a half hour before we came upon a circular object slowly rotating in space. It looked like a giant metal plate, but as we got closer, I could see windows along the edge.

We slowly glided over the top of the space station, and Saranyu's communicator flashed.

"State your Aras credentials," a voice boomed from the communicator.

"Saranyu Gem, Aras Defense Pilot, Officer Number 6137."

"We have no record of your planned visit. What is the situation?"

"Aras is being attacked by an unknown enemy. Defenseless, we have escaped the onslaught, but we fear Aras may be at serious risk. We request to enter the station and contact Aras."

A giant metal door opened to a blue forcefield. Once we reached the inside, the ship landed softly. We opened the doors and stepped out. It was a giant cargo bay with sturdy metallic walls. Ships and iron crates littered the area. It was silent for a few moments. Then a door opened along the back wall.

"Please enter the elevator and choose 'S' floor," beamed a voice through speakers.

We entered a circular glass elevator. We descended into a gigantic open room with big glass windows for walls. The windows provided an exceptional view of space, and the nebulous storm mass in the distance. There were trees growing throughout. They were scrutinized by men and women in white lab coats. When we stepped into the room, all attention fell entirely upon us. A man with short black hair and glasses approached us.

"Hello, I'm Mandell. We are contacting Aras now. Please, follow me to the command centre and we'll try to straighten this out."

We followed him.

"This is quite a station," I said. "What are you studying?"

"We are studying samples of the storm and its interaction with various flora. Aras has been lucky to avoid the storm, for the most part, at least compared to other planets in Archived Thought, however given Aras's orbit and the growing nature of the storm, it's only a matter of time before the planet is fully consumed."

"Are these trees resilient to the storm?"

"No. Even though we have altered their growth to strengthen them, they are still susceptible to consumption by the storm, and eventually will deteriorate."

"If you are studying the relationship between flora and the storm, why have you not placed the station in closer proximity to the storm?"

"The storm is near Aris; however, we can not place the station within the storm as it will break down the composition of the station within a relatively short time."

Cabell paused in contemplation.

"We have some samples that may be of interest to you. In our travels, we found a curious planet, 'Atavika,' which seemed especially resilient to the storm. We met a man, who provided us with samples of the Atavika 'lief, a special plant that grew there. It deflected the storm and shows great promise for future development. We have the samples in our ship."

"We'd be most interested in this," Mandell said.

"And the Marzanna 'lief, as well," I said. "The 'lief best known for adjusting one to the storm and allowing one to transcend it. We have samples of this you may study as well."

"This is excellent," Mandell said.

We reached an office area with many computers, and a communication link to Aras. A blue-uniformed Aras officer looked up and spoke directly to Mandell, with a look of panic.

"It's bad," he said. "The city has lost many turrets and defense ships. The only conciliation is that the attacking fleet has left, but unfortunately it looks like they have pursued the ship with our friends. We may be in danger."

"They want the ship," said Saranyu. "We are a peaceful race. We do not wish battle with them. However, we can not sacrifice the ship without stranding our friends here on Aras, when they wish to return to their homes. Perhaps we can lead them out of Aras, into the storm? It's dangerous, but we must protect Aras. Evasion has been our only ally thus far; their technology is advanced. They are definitely not of our world."

"Agreed," I said. "We've seen their ships; they are identical to ours. Perhaps we can lead them into the storm and escape them for good."

"The ship really appears to bring you somewhere unique to your own desires," said Cabell. "With that type of navigation system, it's probably a safe bet that we can completely throw them off by entering the storm."

"Agreed," said Saranyu. "Let's do it."

"Wait," said the officer at the command station.

"What is it?" Mandell said.

"Sir, we've got a situation here. An anomaly is coming up on the radar. I can't make out what it is, but there are numerous heat signals...right in front of the station?"

We turned and stared out the window. It was eerily quiet and still. I stared into the stars, then I saw something that made my blood run cold. The light from one of the stars in the distance seemed to move slightly.

We had no chance to react as a series of shots fired directly at the window, deflected by a blue forcefield around the station. A couple dozen ships appeared, striking us with an immense laser power.

"I'm guessing they're not willing to chat," Saranyu said.

"There's no telling how long the forcefield will last," said Mandell, as we all ran to the elevator. "This station isn't built for such an assault!"

"Let's get out of here and drive them away," Saranyu said.

The station shook as we rose in the elevator, away from the constant laser-fire of the ships. We made it to the cargo bay and beelined to the ship.

We passed 'lief samples to Mandell, when the metal door shook.

"They made it through the forcefield." Cried Mandell."

"We've got to go. Now." shouted Saranyu.

Mandell ran back to the elevator and Saranyu took the wheel as the cargo bay broke open with laser fire. It fell completely apart. Our ship burst through the rubble and shot out into space, hotly pursued by the fleet.

V

Saranyu's maneuvering of the ship was exceptional, but we couldn't outrun them forever. As she approached Aris, the storm appeared with Aras visible in the distance. We came up on it fast.

"They're gaining on us," Cabell yelled.

"We're almost at the storm," Saranyu said.

As we closed in on the storm, Saranyu began to spin the ship to avoid the fire, but one of the enemies was on our tail.

"Hold tight!"

As we held on to the sides of the ship, she took a sharp left, but hit something. Another ship was right next to us.

The storm closed in fast.

"Look out," Fathom yelled, as the new ship tried to knock us off course.

"I can't turn," Saranyu shouted.

We hit the storm.

SARANYU PILOTS

The cold storm faded leaving me with a warm memory of first days of training. We were so young when they first put us through the academy. The lockers of the old school scrolled through my mind, leading to the hangers, where we spent a good many days learning defensive flight training.

I'd excelled in the computer simulations, and many of the boys had grown quite jealous, some even attempting to thwart my progress. But I couldn't be stopped.

Was this my first day of actual flight training? In the hanger, my instructor sat in the pilot's seat of the first ship I'd ever piloted. As I walked up to him, he jumped out of the ship and removed his helmet. I expected his calm but stern face with that tangly black hair, but instead I was faced with an older man with a graying beard. The man smiled at me. How strange. Who was this man?

"No matter what, Saranyu, in the end, remember to follow your heart," the man said, and he threw his hand out for me. I reached out and he helped pull me up into the ship. Together, we flew off into the turbulence of the storm.

SULLAMECHA
WITH: SARANYA

I

We slowed rotation from the spin as we departed the intergalactic portal of the storm. The ship thrust through space at a rapid pace. Such a clever ship; the steering was highly responsive, allowing it pull off evasive maneuvers I'd never thought possible.

An orange and red hued planet grew before us, glowing an intense neon. It brought to mind the brilliant flash of the flares we had shot when surrendering during a training exercise. A sun in the distance was setting it aglow. I slowly brought the ship into orbit, and we approached the atmosphere carefully.

I'd been to many planets within our solar system, but this was unlike any I'd visited before. As we dropped closer to the surface, the bright orange glow dampened to reveal a dusty beige that permeated the entire surface with a familiar undulation of a desert.

"It worked," said Cabell. "Looks like we've lost them."

"Yes, but this planet doesn't look especially hospitable," Nivea said.

She was right. As we descended, it was clear that this

was a hot, dry desert planet with many sand dunes. I recalled my years of training as a pilot on Aris. The military freight hauler that brought us there was slow, but Aris's gray deserts were a sandbox of fun.

We cruised over the dunes for a good twenty minutes without finding any signs of life, but we did find a curious anomaly: a bump in the sand, with an opening. We decided to land the ship and investigate. I pulled back on the wheel to reduce the thrust, landing it in the sand close to the anomaly.

Outside of the ship, it was incredibly hot and sweat ran down my forehead. A gentle breeze brushed my face and blew against my brown hair. I reached down to feel the sand. Its warmth seemed to swell in my hands. The grains were very fine, and the sand fell through my fingers.

"If there's any source of water, this would be a pretty habitable planet," said Nivea.

"It's likely that there are some water sources. Look at that," I said, pointing towards a smaller spiky cactus at the bottom edge of the dune. Fathom walked down the dune and went to touch it.

"Be careful," Cabell said. "Those spikes can do you some damage. Cacti may be lush with life, but from the outside they are potentially deadly."

We walked down the dune heading to the area we'd spotted from the ship. It was the opening of a cave. We carefully edged our way inside. It was so dark; we couldn't see anything. Nivea produced a fire which cast a light over the space, revealing a small mechanical device. It was only about as big as a suitcase.

Upon close inspection it looked like it had an engine attached to the back of it. In the front, there was a black screen which stared back at us. Whatever it was, it wasn't active, at least it didn't appear to be. I knelt down and stared into the glass. I could see my long brown hair and blue eyes in the reflection.

"It looks like there may be a presence here after all," I said. "Although, just what kind, it's hard to say."

A small red light appeared on the machine's screen. We stared at it. A bright white light flashed there, and the small device shot to life, wings shooting out of the sides of it. We ran out of the cave, but it followed us, flying at an aggressive rate. It shot red lasers at us as we ran up the dune, but we managed to close the ship's door before being shot.

It continued shooting at us, knocking the ship back and forth, so we quickly ignited the ship thrusting ourselves up into the air, in an attempt to evade it.

"It's some sort of defense drone," Nivea said, as we raced over the sand dunes, the drone still shooting at us at every turn. I swerved to avoid the fire, but when we were forced to absorb the shots, there didn't appear to be substantial damage done to the ship. It was sturdy, for sure. Most likely some sort of shield was protecting us.

The robot proved to be clever, though. Its movements were like no AI I'd faced before. We were at a loss as to how to escape it, and we really had nowhere to take cover.

We were about to ascend into space, when several dark objects appeared on the horizon. As we came closer, it was clearly a city, but with old ironclad buildings covered in sand. It looked inactive, as though it had been vacated a long time ago.

I took the opportunity to evade the drone by swerving around the dull gray-black buildings. Still, it was incredibly difficult to shake off my tail. I made a quick turn around one massive building, and then another, and again. We were now flying in a slightly different direction, and it appeared as though we had left it in the dust, for now. We had the speed advantage.

I darted my eyes left and right looking for a way to exit the village without arising the suspicion of the drone. Surely, it would see us if we rose. I made the decision to park the ship in an alley tucked between two bigger buildings, and we waited.

"Curious," said Cabell. "It definitely looks like this place has been abandoned."

"Yes," I said. "And they appear to be impervious to entry. I haven't seen any windows or doors, it's like they're just deadweight, or locked shut. Highly fortified."

"Would it kill us to explore a little?" Nivea asked.

"It very well could," said Fathom. "This place hasn't been too friendly thus far."

"Don't be silly," I said. "There's nothing wrong with exploring around the ship a little."

With that I opened the door and stepped out. The air was a lot danker here. The buildings were high, but not as high as they were on Aras. Though they were, without a doubt, incredibly durable. I walked up and touched one with my hand. It was dry and matte but did offer a dull shine.

The others joined me as I walked along the side of a building. I found a small opening which led downwards along a slight decline. I looked down into the space to see a glossy object reflecting light. The area appeared to be safe, so I began to head down.

"Be careful," Cabell said.

"It's fine," I said. "There's nothing down here."

Despite my confident display there was an unusual quietness to the area, and I wondered if we were being watched. When I reached the object at the end of the small decline, I could see it was a sort of glass circle embedded into the building, built into a larger circular space that possibly could be a door. As I stared into sphere, I once again recognized my reflection. Cautiously, I reached out to touch the object.

As with the drone, there was a flash and a red light that grew from within the shiny globe. I fell back on the ground. The light did not stop there, though, it ran along the edges of the building in diverting lines, like blood flowing in the veins of some hidden beast.

I promptly jumped to my feet and called to the others to go back to the ship. As we ran, the red lights blazed across the city walls as if we'd excited some dormant monster.

"Run," I cried, a sense of impending doom gripping my stomach. We jumped into the ship, and though there was no apparent threat, the walls were glowing bright red.

Suspecting there may be imminent danger, I thrust the ship up into the air and we began dashing through the city walls. And that's when we saw them. A swarm of drones appearing above the city. Then, they were appearing left and right, behind us, down every corridor. The damn drones were everywhere! They quickly closed in us with their blood-red eyes and startling accuracy.

We would give them a good run. Finding a long stretch, I thrust the ship ahead as fast as I could muster, and we were able to swerve around the appearing drones. They loomed above in the star filled sky, and I feared that we could not keep this up for too long.

"Look," cried Fathom. He was pointing along the alleyways to the right which, through intermittent glimpses, we could see the desert sand once again. There were no drones in the desert.

I slowed enough for the drones to catch up and although our ship took another shot, we made a quick turn and blasted into the desert.

The city disappeared behind us, and we once again surfed the dunes of the desert. But almost as quickly as we'd entered the desert, the sand gave way to rocky, mountainous terrain. Cliffs rose high into the air—we were in a massive chasm that grew deeper and more enclosed. We had no space to move.

"They're still chasing us," cried Nivea, who was looking through the side window.

"Look," cried Fathom. A quick glance to the side of the chasm revealed pathways and larger pieces of machinery strewn along cliffside. Almost immediately, one began shooting at us. Turrets.

Gigantic robots stood up. They fired at us with red lasers, with a stupefying accuracy. Our plight had quickly become desperate. We could not travel up as the top of the cavern was closed off with ledges. We had to keep moving forward.

Drones appeared from the cracks of the chasm. They fired with a steadfast determination. I realized I could not overcome the firepower. We had to land somewhere, now!

We dove down further into the chasm. The path forward became rockier and more enclosed. A laser shot set us into a spiral and I tried to steady us, but we veered off course and knocked into a ledge. The ship bounced to the side, then hit a rocky surface, skidding before crashing to a halt.

II

The ship wouldn't restart. The turrets were still firing at us, pushing our ship off the ledge. There was an open cave to our left. Given the volatility of the shots, we made the decision to ditch the ship and run for shelter.

We dashed through the laser fire into the cave's opening. Having escaped the onslaught of lasers, we took a moment to look around the cave. There was no other trace of human life. It was small, but the back appeared to go on for a while into darkness.

"What now?" Cabell asked.

"I'm betting those drones won't have too much trouble finding us," I said. "Quick, head into the dark and hide, if you can."

We hustled to the back of the cave. The lasers were still shooting at the ship outside, and we feared an attack from the flying drones.

"Wait," Cabell said. "Right here, there is a very narrow

crack in the wall. And…is that a dim light back there?"

We moved over closer to Cabell, and indeed, there was a dim light visible through a very small crack in the wall.

"Kick it, punch it, whatever you have to do, break it open so we can fit through."

Outside, we could hear the drones swarming around the ship. We each took turns beating at the crack in the wall, and eventually it gave way enough for Cabell to fit through. We followed him, and soon we were in a narrow hallway leading to a dim light at the end.

The laser fire died down as we progressed further into the cave. Reaching the end of the hall, Fathom knocked his foot on some sort of cargo box. At first, we thought it was locked, but it opened to reveal a big electronic device.

"Strange," Cabell said. "It almost looks like a giant battery, but for what? The robots outside?"

We roamed for some time, before reaching a bigger room with terminals built into the walls. There was broken robotics machinery strewn about, similar to what we'd encountered outside. As well, there were two walls which were of a similar dull metallic substance to the buildings of the city, and they contained the globes we'd seen earlier. They were doorways, maybe, but they were closed.

"Curious technology," Cabell said.

The buzz of drones and laser-fire could became louder. The drones had entered the cave.

"What do we do?" Nivea cried.

We looked at each other. The lasers continued.

"Somehow they know we're in here," Fathom cried.

"This is bad," Nivea said.

We exchanged dashed glances. In a fit of anxiety, I

jumped over to one of the globe doors. I placed my hand up against the globe, which instantly lit up with a red light, just like before. I pulled my hand back quick, and the screen flashed to life. The familiar red veins flushed out over the entire door.

"What have you done?" cried Cabell.

The door opened, and a giant mechanical creature immerged, shooting lasers at us. Nivea was hit, then Cabell. Fathom and I ran down the hallway only to be hit by a laser as well. I held my leg in pain and looked up to see the first drone approaching from the cave before I blacked out.

III

I awoke to blurry lights rising above. I was dropping. I could feel that we were falling, fast. I squirmed, but I was bound to some sort of gurney. The lights kept strobing over my face and, with my eyes closed, it felt as if they were probing into my mind.

I opened my eyes and turned my head to see the others who were also incapacitated. There, next to us, were two giant robots just like the one that had opened up the door and shot at us. I tried to speak, but my mouth was bound.

The strobing lights gave way to darkness. Then, slowly, rock stalactites came into view, and a cavern appeared through a window. Extremely high computer terminals were stacked inside. Robots and androids stared at me. The vision lasted briefly before disappearing into darkness again.

After about five minutes the door opened. The robots

next to me pushed me into a dark room, then left me and the others there.

The light increased slowly, attenuating brighter until it filled the entire room. There was medical supplies and machinery, but no scientists. There were operating tables all around, but no doctors. What kind of creepy operation room was this?

Two figures moved towards us. Androids. Highly sophisticated humanoid creatures with white strips instead of eyes, silvery metallic heads and speakers for mouths. As I struggled to move, one of their white light strips flashed, scanning me.

"Relax, Saranyu," one of them said. The audio beamed through the oval speaker on their head where a human mouth would be.

"Yes, relax fighter," the other said.

"You are quite an evasive pilot," the first android continued. "Your friends here have not yet woken, yet here you are, already trying to escape. Don't bother. It isn't possible. You're in a highly secure vault facility quite far from any other organic life forms."

"How do you know my name?" The light flashed again.

"We know your name through a simple temporal lobe scan. A full brain scan will tell us more about your origins. You will be sedated for this scan."

I struggled to no avail.

"Just relax, Saranyu. You have no recourse. You will be sedated. Once we find what we need to know, your fate will be determined, as will the fate of your friends."

I struggled in vain as an android brought a needle to

my neck and pierced my flesh.

A woozy, disoriented vision appeared. I was veering left and right, but after an extended period of nausea and dizziness, my shaking head steadied, and through a blurry fog my familiar cockpit came into view. The windshield sparkled with bright beams of sunlight.

"They're attacking! Throw them off." The command came from my headset, the voice was a commander I'd who trained me, his voice always carried stressed orders even in the tamest of situations.

I looked at the radar to see that we were being followed by several triangular ships like the ones that had attacked us on Aras. I dove into a tailspin to evade them, which was effective, but we were outnumbered. We could only keep this up for so long.

After a series of successful evasive moves, I took on fire, and my aircraft dove towards the water. I ejected with my parachute, and when I finally hit the water, I detached my parachute and began swimming.

My desperate swim ended when I found a beach. I stumbled out of the water and fell into eerily familiar soft sand. I twisted my head up to see that I was on an island just like that of the virtual reality training island on Aras. We had been given many training missions on this island, and I knew it inside out. I'd always had a fondness for it, but never actually existed on Aras, it was only a simulation.

In the sky above I could see several black and silver ships attacking, the same ones from my recent memory. One shot down at me. I ran into a nearby woods, finding refuge in a cave.

No sooner did I step in the cave then the entrance disappeared, and I was forced to walk further into the cave. I entered a room with a light that grew from above. The room was full of broken robot parts. I jumped back, falling onto my backside, as a man stepped into the light. He was tall and thin with long messy hair, a kempt beard and notable red eyes. There was something off about him.

"You are quite the pilot," he said, staring at me with a pensive gaze. He spoke absently, but his eyes seemed to penetrate mind. "We share the same enemy."

"Who are you?" I demanded.

He paused, as if carefully considering what to say.

"Call me Dem. You know, you are awfully lucky to have found yourself in the hands of a benevolent race."

I looked at him apprehensively. I did not yet trust him. I recalled our capture and the elevator ride. I needed to know more.

"Benevolent is a pretty funny word to use for what we've experienced so far. Are you behind these androids that sedated me?"

The man walked over to a broken android, knelt, then pulled it up to face him.

"Ah, the APEX model. Yes, it's one of the better models, for sure. There are many capable androids. The ones you met were in charge of sedation and brain scan technology. We have the power to insert this technology into any organic or inorganic matter."

"They were quite rude. And you're not much better. Could you kindly explain what the hell is going on?"

"Look, we're not sure how much *we* can trust *you*

yet."

"Are you joking? You capture me and my friends, you sedate us with God-knows-what, you infiltrate our minds. What do you hope to accomplish?"

"Look, I know you're upset, but we have to take serious precautions against our adversaries. If you're not connected to them, you should take the same precautions."

"Who the hell are they?"

The man stood up again and walked over closer to me, his red eyes glowed as his gaze locked on me.

"They are an extremely violent race set on colonizing the universe for their own gain, at any cost. They destroyed most of our great city and they have attacked our planet multiple times in an attempt to steal our technology. They won't get it though, not as long as we're alive."

"And *who*, exactly, are *you*?"

"You may call us the Sulla. We were once a great civilization. Now we are the remnants of that. We are developing a new technology capable of leaving this planet, finding our adversary in their home world, and fighting them in retribution for the pain and loss they have caused. With the exponential rate our technology is growing, that will one day be possible. For now, we're hiding from them."

"How are you talking to me in this dream?"

"That's enough about us. How did *you* get here?"

I paused, glaring at him. There was no way he was going to tell me more, I knew that. Given that I was completely at his mercy, it was just as well I was forthright.

"My friends and I, we came from a planet called Aras. My civilization is technologically savvy as well, but our skill is in ship building. We build powerful spaceships, and we have explored far in our galaxy."

"Intriguing," Dem said, with an apparent genuine interest. "But we have seen the ship you came in; it is the
ship of our alien adversaries. How is this so?"

I considered this. So, the spaceship we had, it was of
the hostile alien race. The technology belonged to them.
This made a lot of sense, given our experience with the
fleet that attacked us.

"This ship was found by my friends, on a planet far
away called *Earth*," I said. "They received this ship before
they travelled to me. The ship has a technology that can
travel through the storm…"

"Storm? What storm?"

"The…storm. You don't know of the storm?"

"We do not know of it."

"There is a storm that is ravishing the universe. It is
near your planet, and one day it may consume it."

"The anomaly? Oh…yes. We know of this. However,
we have never studied it with great intensity. It has never
actually breached the atmosphere. You are saying that it
acts as a sort of, portal, for space travel?"

"Yes. And communication across great distances."

"Incredible. We watched you from when you first landed on the planet. Your piloting abilities are very strong.
Your race must be very proud. Well, Saranyu, although
my colleagues are very weary of your entry in the ship,
your intentions seem innocent as far as I can see. I will be
vouching for your freedom, but it's unlikely the masters
will allow you free anytime soon. We'll do the best we can
to get you out of here as soon as possible."

"You're telling me that you're going to keep us trapped

here?"

"Your fate is beyond my control. I will try the best I can. Look, most likely you will be listed as a minor risk, and you will be given a temporary freedom on our android deck, where you will be fed and live fairly peacefully for the time being. However, this floor is restricted and under our control, so you won't be able to escape it. I have to go now. I hope to meet with you again, soon."

I felt the dream subside into darkness.

IV

I awoke, again, in the hands of androids. This time however, we were confined to bedrooms. The androids fed us, and we were cared for like sick children. I had a feeling that we were being watched and assessed.

A few days passed like this, before we were finally allowed to leave the confines of the sleeping quarters, and we were permitted onto a giant floor stacked with machines and electronics that was maintained by the androids. They allowed us to explore, but we wore bracelets which would stun us if we tried to leave. Not that we could leave anyway, the doors were highly secure.

We had gotten used to our new home and even grown friendly with the surprisingly lifelike androids. Then one day we were called to a room of computers, where we were instructed to lie down on soft cushy beds and close our eyes. The beds slid back into a wall, and we were instantly whisked away to a virtual reality, where we were trained on how to operate spacecraft. My trainer was Dem, and he was incredibly diligent instructing me on how to fly their virtual drones and mecha robots.

It was a walk in the park for me. I was mesmerized with how intelligent Dem was. He knew everything about drone operation, right down to the intricate circuits that allowed them to operate. We learned how to fly them, we learned how to shoot enemies, we learned how to stealthily collect information and we learned how to pulverize the enemy with a suicide move; one that sent a pulse of electricity out over a network rendering it inactive, while completely deleting the content of the drone.

The exercises grew old, but we had grown great friends with the androids. Although we were led to believe that the androids were autonomous, there was doubt amongst us, but we never fully articulated it, suspecting that we were being watched constantly.

The robots were definitely self-sufficient, but the androids appeared almost too life-like at times, and we suspected they were being controlled by some other entity, but there were no clues provided as to just whom that entity might be.

Then there was Dem and a few other 'virtual illusions' who professed to be programs, but would not go into any details on the great civilization that once existed on Sullamecha. There was something suspect about it.

Regardless, they were essentially friendly, although they said they couldn't let us go until they were sure we could be trusted. The ship that we'd come in had been taken and quarantined, and the technology was being studied. We didn't mind; again, we didn't really have much choice in the matter.

One day, we were interrupted from our virtual training by an ominous alert.

"We have spotted numerous unidentified objects incoming," Dem said, interrupting my drone navigation simulation. "We've got Tier 1 drones on it, but they're being overtaken. We're going to link you up to real-time Tier 2 robots, we need your help in taking them down, Saranyu. There are a lot of them."

"Why are we only hearing of this now?"

"We are only aware of it just now. I'm linking you up immediately. Saranyu, remember, no matter what, I'll be here the background to help. Okay?"

"Okay."

My vision blurred and then adjusted to a bright, white light which dialed back to darkness. I initiated a launch sequence and sent a sleeper drone up into the air, thrusting it left and right through a narrow cave and out into the bright sunlight of the dunes of Sullamecha.

The radar indicated there was a fleet of ships attacking from above. This was bad. I lifted the drone up into the air and fired on every ship I could. I successfully took down three or four before I sustained significant damage and took a nose-dive into the ground.

I switched to another drone and rose it from its sleeper cave. I managed to destroy another three enemy ships before my sleeper drone was taken down. This was not a drill; my success had been a lot better in virtual reality.

I repeated this for another good five or six drones, before I heard Dem speak to me from the background.

"Good Saranyu, but we've got another fleet following them and the drones are not cutting it. We're going to have to move to the Tier 3 robot-operated ships. Are you ready?"

"Never more ready," I said.

I felt the vision shift to a robot's eyes in a sophisticated ship. This was more like it. The Sulla had a whole army of android ships attacking, but there was no defence like a human-guided ship.

Navigating a hidden cave location, I burst out into the chasm with lasers already firing at the ships I'd been tracking by radar. They didn't last long. I took down five at the same time, then plowed on through another three before sustaining significant damage, but I evaded the attack and did a nosedive downward, going head over heels before flying back up and twisting around to fake the fleet out. I managed to take out another seven ships before my ship took fatal damage.

"Great job," Dem said.

I switched to another ship and began attacking again. With the others, we managed to take out most of the fleet. But Dem spoke to me again from the background.

"Saranyu, you've done good but we need you to disengage."

"What? No! I've taken out nearly the whole fleet!"

"Saranyu, you need to disengage now, or we will force you to."

"Why the hell would you?"

"There are multiple fleets approaching the planet. This is very bad. We don't have the capacity for—"

"No, I can take them. All of us working together, we can—"

"I'm not going ask you again."

I glanced at the radar. There were no more ships visible, but the radar did not span far beyond the planet. Dem had a broader view. There was no reason to doubt him. But then, weren't we good enough to take them? There were several of us were prepared for—"

My vision became blurry.

I awoke shaking on the bed in the computer room with the others standing around me.

"We have orders to move to a safer area," Cabell said. "The androids will take us. It's looking really bad. They're not sure if—"

"I almost had them," I yelled.

"Saranyu," Nivea screamed. "We have to get to safety. It sounds really bad."

I turned to two androids that were coming towards and gesturing for us to follow. Jarring back to reality, I ran with the others.

V

We ran to the elevator and began descending with our four android chaperones. The floors that flew past us appeared to show more electronic storage, wires, and mainframes. We descended many floors before the lights dimmed and we were left in darkness.

The androids operated the control panel to the elevator to no avail.

"This is not a good sign," Cabell said.

We waited for a good thirty minutes, before there was a loud banging coming from outside the elevator.

"What the hell is it?" Fathom said.

We stood silent, until the impact became visible on the

side of the elevator. Then we screamed.

The androids again fiddled with the control panel, and prepared their lasers. Hesitantly, they gave us spare laser-guns they had hidden.

When the side of the elevator split open, we jumped back against the opposite wall and the androids shot madly at the hole that had opened. Whoever was trying to break in must have been stunned by that attack, but quickly laser shots followed from outside and the iron of the elevator was torn open.

We knelt down for protection as the laser-fire raced on like a game of quantum ping pong. Two androids dropped in the crossfire and the other two slid down to a sitting position, still firing.

"Run," the androids said, as it became clear our attackers were not ceasing. Surveying the outside area, we could see our attackers were approaching from the long end of a cavernous terrain, and the androids had successfully kept them at quite a distance.

We had enough room to run for a nearby maintenance hallway. In the moment we were exposed to high temperatures, I could see our attackers out of the corner of my eye. They were tall and wore gray suits. Their heads were protected by glass helmets and were much bigger than any humans would be. Their skin looked to be black.

We dove through the hot cavern and into the hallway which was absent of attackers. It appeared to be some sort of facility service hallway, as if it were meant for the upkeep of the base exterior and was not for regular use. It was lit by an electronic light and covered with metal panels. The aliens saw us and attacked, but not in time to be able to hit us. We ran down the hallway.

An alien shot a panel causing it to spray electrical ash. It was overwhelmingly hot. The laser-fire continued behind us, and Fathom and Nivea fired back when they could, but for the most part we just ran as fast as possible.

The race continued into a brighter area with a glass walkway. Outside there was strangely reddish substance, it was like lava but thinner. The temperature was so high that a human would not survive long, whereas an android could last much longer.

The aliens did not stop their pursuit. We fired several shots then crossed the glass walkway. Just after turning a corner at the end of the hallway, we heard a crash.

"They destroyed the walkway," Nivea shouted.

We continued running into another cavernous area until we reached a door that would not open, despite our screams.

I saw a globe and pressed it with my hand. A red light appeared within the globe, but it just remained there. The door did not open.

"The destroyed walkway should hold them," said Cabell, "but perhaps not for long. We need to get in."

Our screams grew more desperate as we continued knocking on the door. Finally, the door burst open, and we jumped inside. It closed and locked, as if operated by some higher power.

The room we now found ourselves in was curious. There were monitors showing many different areas of the underground facility. It seemed to be some sort of security station. The computer interfaces were unusual though. Most of the interfaces around the underground facility were direct links which robots operated by physically linking up to and were inoperable by humans. The interfaces in this room were much more human-friendly.

"Look," shouted Cabell, pointing at a monitor that showed another cavernous area that appeared to be a bay of fighter ships and drones. One in particular stood out. It was our ship.

"They must have held it for study," Nivea said.

"By the looks of these security cameras, there may be a crack in the ceiling leading up to the surface for the drones. So, if we can get to the ship, we should be able to get it out of here. How can we get to it?"

"Look," I said, pointing at the left wall. "There's a map of this area. If we take the next left service hall, it should take us right to it."

The aliens hit the door with lasers.

"We've got to go, now." Nivea said.

"I can buy us some time," I said, opening a virtual reality bed and jumping in. "Push me in the wall, they'll never know I'm here. I'll be able to operate the drones and give you cover to the ship."

"That's dangerous," said Cabell. Are you sure?

"Of course, I'm sure. You want to get back to earth, don't you? You need me to buy you extra time so you can get to that pilot's seat, Cabell. It's so close, all you have to do is get into the ship's bay, and I'll easily cover you. There's no way they'll be able to get you with me protecting. Don't worry about me, I'll be fine.

Will Saranyu go or will Cabell pilot?

Saranyu Goes   Cabell Pilots
Continue Reading   Go to Page 197

SARANYA GOES

A laser ripped through the door.

"We've got to go," screamed Nivea, grabbing my arm. We dashed through the second entrance, down the hall until we broke into the bay area with the other ships. The aliens burst in.

"There it is," I shouted, pointing at the ship. We ran to it and opened the doors and I jumped inside as the lasers came closer.

I took the wheel but was immediately torn from it by a figure outside the ship. The figure shot the others and threw me into the passenger seat.

I looked up to see the ship moving. It burst through glass into a cavernous area with the reddish lava-like substance, and then up, up through a crevice in the ceiling.

Another of the many worlds we've travelled, for that foolish creature and his stupid furry face, and here, our ship is in the hands of a known enemy.

But no more. We have the ship. We're in the storm. Heading home. No more will the ship be in the hands of a boundless fool.

The image of him is out there, somewhere, pale and pathetic, begging for the ship back, begging for our acquiescence, helplessly trying to reason, but despite our efforts, despite our numerous attempts to find him, we've come up empty handed.

Regardless, we have regained the ship. Our mission is complete.

UNKNOWN STARSHIP
WITH: UNKNOWN PILOT

I entered the landing bay at impulse power. Stabilization completed. Forcefield powered off. Shields were down. The landing was successful.

I stepped out into the familiar oxygenated bay of our ship. Our fleet joined me, each ship landing one at a time from space. A veteran pilot, my old friend, stepped up to me, his black tentacles capped by his helmet.

"Are they out?" he asked.

"They're stunned. Bound, captive, secure in the ship."

"Take one of them and report to command with news of the successful mission."

I opened the back door of the ship and pulled one of the unconscious aliens up into my arms, her long brown hair falling to the side.

We approached the storm teleporters. Channelling through the storm we arrived at the main bridge. My companions greeted our arrival with tentacle nods indicative of a successful mission.

"How long since the last communication with the League," I asked.

"Five days. You have been gone for nineteen days."

I walked around the deck observing our crew who were of excited in reception of our arrival.

"Have there been battles?"

"One battle, an inferior race miscalculated our dominance, their ship was quickly obliterated. We had to fly through a benign civilization in chase with the ship. The pilot was formidable."

The bridge screen provided a view of our current location, a destination quite far from our homeland. The exploration in our absence had yielded no suitable planets for settlement, otherwise we would have begun colonization.

"Any new notes on exploration?"

"None. We explored a planet which showed potential, but quickly became a false hope when scientific tests indicated the storm gains virulence when exposed to the atmosphere. It nearly cut through our suit technology. We aborted the mission immediately."

"Any word from homeland?"

"They are awaiting your arrival. They are in disarray. The storm has rendered the planet nearly uninhabitable; all remaining species are being transported to suspended animation in space where possible."

I turned to a nearby aid, passing the alien thief to him. "Revive her. We will bring her through the gate."

We entered a dark room with the storm-gate machines. We hooked our minds up to the system waiting for the familiar wash of information to flow over us as we connected to the storm, our bodies shook with an overwhelming amount of pain and pleasure.

And we were in. Homeland was in the forefront, ravished by the storm since our departure, it was painful to see. My mind's eye fell upon a group of faces superimposed upon the image of our homeland. On the periphery the other planets of the Defense League remained attentive as the League Master spoke.

"We have been advised your mission has been successful and the entirety of the Defense League is thankful. The Science League is of excited to learn that the storm-force ship technology has been successful in achieving universal travel. We will be holding a celebration in the next month to honor you with the highest notch for bravery. Please disclose now your details of the mission."

"Travel was not easy. We landed on many worlds irrelevant to our objective, and some worlds in which we only just missed the thief. Many worlds were habitable, providing promise for colonization."

The minds of the others buzzed with unique new fires, their ideas swirling in thought columns that I did not choose to explore at the time.

"We did not find the original thief, but through concentrated focus of his travels, we tracked him to a planet named Marzanna. *A connection here led us to a world named* Aras, *a unique planet ripe with alien creatures of considerable intelligence, but little threat. We explored the planet and found them in a city. They escaped to a nearby space station, but we did not catch up to them in time due the maneuvering of a formidable pilot.*

"We spent the remaining days trying to catch up with the thief to no avail. We found many unique worlds, but no imprint of their presence in the storm. It seemed as though they'd escaped off the radar of the storm.

"Then, we picked up a bizarre biological heat signal on Sul-lamecha, *the potential settlement we have been pursuing for quite a while, which is home to a highly intelligent species that has built up a technological barrier that we've been trying to destroy for ages."*

"We touched down on the alien, desert landscape to fight off the usual aerial attacks, but we followed the heat signals down deep into the planet's underground, where we infiltrated an android-built defense and found the prisoners and the ship there. We have brought the female alien pilot for your consideration."

"You may revive her," The League Master said.

I broke from the storm long enough to revive the alien woman and connect her to the storm. She woke, opening her consciousness to us for exploration. Immediately we perused her mind looking for more information about the original alien thief and the nature of this alien's native world. As she woke within the storm, her eyes darted madly around, a normal response for a novice in the storm.

"What is this," she cried.

"Alien woman, your name we find in your consciousness to be... 'Saranyu,' your kind has engaged in terrorism by taking possession of our highly sensitive technology, the damage caused is potentially unknowable from this vantage point."

Saranyu blinked, looking around, unable to penetrate the mind defenses we had now raised as a result of her cognizance. Then, seeming to come to grips with the apparent insanity of her situation, she spoke again.

"You are a species that has captured us? What are your demands? We mean no harm."

"You are an inferior species," the League Master said. "But you are of close competence. Your air force capabilities are of interest to us. You will be compliant in advising us of your defense methods against the storm."

"We will not comply with tyranny. What are your intentions?"

"Our intentions are that which we carry on now," the Master said. "We will be visiting your world again, with your help. You will be giving us information, that we are now obtaining from your mind, that will lead to the successful colonization of our species in a new habitable world, at any cost."

"We will never bow to tyranny," Saranyu said.

"You can and you will. We have captured enough of you to explore new worlds in the storm, based on your unique biochemical anatomies. Within each of your individual minds, there is endless potential for exploration of worlds beyond our area of the universe. Your capture has opened the door to an entirely new dimension of space travel never before known."

"We will never comply. We will fight."

I ignored her foolish pleas and reached into her subconscious for any information that might give us insight into potential planetary settlements, especially with regards to Sullamecha, the planet where we found her.

This planet was one of the best options for settlement as it was within the same galaxy as our homeland, it contained many resources, and fell at a very low probability of storm consumption. At the same time it remained in close proximity to the storm.

I dove into her subconsciousness, where I became audience at a small island with ships flying overhead. It was an island that seemed to resonate with her youth. I followed her knowledge in the form of her self as she explored the island, and came face to face with a man of curious existence. His face looked of *alien life, but there was much more standing up behind him. He was like a wall of information. I could sense something beyond him that was highly defended by a wall of technology.*

As they began to talk, I tried to push against the man's façade to discover if his location was on Sullamecha. At first, I was unable to. But I began to make progress slowly. As I pried, he picked up a broken android, explaining something about its defenses, and suddenly he smiled a knowing smile, his red eyes glaring at me as the android flashed..."

I was shaken out of the storm by another.

"What is it?" I shouted.

"Our defenses have been compromised! There's been some sort of electronic surge! We are powerless!"

I jumped up and ran to the bridge. There was no power.

"Why aren't we on backup power?"

"There's nothing! We've already tried."

I paused.

"Get that alien woman out of the storm!" I shouted. "Subdue her!"

The crew did as asked, and after a good amount of work, the tech division managed to revive the ship.

"There is unauthorized movement of a ship in the landing bay."

"Turn on the force-fields!" I yelled.

We brought an image of the landing bay on screen just in time to see the recovered ship leave through the undefended landing bay door.

CABELL PILOTS

The familiar deathly cold raged through me, but I overcame it. Now, my veins flowed with a beauty unlike I'd known before.

In front of me, brilliant waterfalls rained down on placid lakes. Colossal skyscrapers dazzled in radiant sunlight. Verdant forests grew with an undying ferocity. The images flushed over me one after the other as if testing my capacity for awe. They were like earth before the storm, but there were many otherworldly variations.

The images continued to cycle, until one stayed. It was a snowclad forest, with a city in the distance. I watched from a mountain as a familiar traveler on a snowy mountain trail sauntered through the forest. Behind him, a city was vaguely visible through the throes of the storm. With his snowy beard and Santa hat, it was clearly Hylotz. I waved at him and he waved back, but he appeared resolute, like he had made a heavily weighed decision. It was the first time I'd seen him unhappy.

In a moment, he turned away from the city and back towards the forest and continued down the path. His footprints wove back and forth erratically like they had when we had first tried to find him.

Ahead of him on the trail, there was a flash of light, and he disappeared in the storm.

PART 5
TERRA BETA
WITH: CABELL

I

We emerged from the tangled web of the storm, the ship weaving left and right through a desperate darkness like a rain-soaked leaf. Where were we now?

The steering wheel shook against my wrist as a new planet appeared through the darkness, its gray inhospitable alien atmosphere was hardly a welcome sight for its weary guests.

"Pull up," Fathom yelled, just before we slammed into the dusty surface, bouncing against the alien regolith multiple times before skidding to a stop.

Through the window, the terrain was clearly uninhabitable. It stretched out to the horizon. Bleak and desolate, it was more akin to the moon than Earth. This seemed to fly in the face of our theory about the ship's ability to travel to destinations of our innermost desires. When I took the wheel, I focused heavily on Earth, so how did we end up in this alien place?

"Not looking too friendly," Fathom said. "Should we get out and explore?"

"Absolutely not," I ordered. "Don't open that door. The absence of stars suggests a depleted atmosphere. You wouldn't last fifteen seconds without losing consciousness."

Fathom frowned. "Well, what now?"

I paused. The most obvious solution would be to take off again, if possible, to give it another shot. The harsh conditions of the planet suggested it simply wasn't worth the stay.

"Cabell, why don't you try piloting us out of here?" said Nivea. "Maybe our next stop will be brighter."

"It's really our only option," I replied. "Okay, lets give it another go."

I grabbed the steering wheel and waited for it to connect to my pulse. Nothing.

"Are you grabbing it tight?" said Fathom.

"I am. The damn thing isn't connecting."

"With that landing…I hate to ask this but, is it broken?"

I paused. With great disdain I was forced to digest that unfortunate truth. I made several other attempts to initialize the launch, to no avail.

"Well?" Fathom asked.

I felt like my whole life on Earth flashed before my eyes. Decades of research papers. Environmental tests. All the excitement of site visits, was it all for this? To be stuck on some lonely, uninhabitable planet at the desolate edge of the universe, left to die in a tiny vessel? Was this the fate of joining with the others to try to help some old homeless guy?

"I'm afraid we're trapped," I replied.

II

We were on our second day of being trapped without

food and we had only limited water. Fathom stared hopelessly out the window. Nivea had resorted to obsessive introversion which was unhelpful. She was obviously accustomed to being connected to the storm on any whim.

"I could really use a smoke," Fathom said, pulling something out of his pocket. "Cabell," he asked, "remember when we were on the island, and we smoked the Ondas 'lief?"

"Yes," I replied.

"It helped us breathe, didn't it? Underwater?"

I paused to consider this. Indeed, the Ondas 'lief appeared to have oxidizing properties. It could help humans breathe underwater. Could it possibly help humans breathe in harsh oxygen-absent environments like this one?

"It's seems pretty risky," said Fathom, "but could it possibly let us breathe outside the ship?

"It's...plausible," I said.

"We don't have many options left at this point," said Nivea. "The Breaus have seen many planets through the eyes of civilizations, and we have seen many utilize the power of 'liefs to their advantage."

"It's crazy...but you're right, we don't really have any other choice," I said. "We'd starve to death if we choose to do nothing."

Nivea prepared the Ondas 'lief for smoking. "Now, what if we add this?" she said, pulling out some Marzanna 'liefs as well. "If we encounter the storm, we'll be able to connect and maybe gain some more insight into our situation." She prepared the 'liefs and provided us each with a joint. We smoked.

Fathom stared out the window. "Well, if this doesn't work, it was nice knowing you," he said.

"It's our only hope. If it works, this could open the door to some interesting scientific possibilities."

Fathom looked at me with a stronger resolve, with his anxiety calmed by the 'lief. With no hesitation, he reached toward the door to open it.

"It's been a blast," he said, and he opened the door.

Struggling to breathe, we passed out.

III

When I came to, the door was open. The others were not in the ship.

"Cabell," Fathom yelled. "Come out here."

I opened my door and jumped outside. The soil was a dark gray, much like the moon's regolith, and the blackness of space made me feel woozy.

"Well, we're still alive, so obviously the Ondas 'lief works," I said. Nivea stood behind me, pointing.

"Take a look, Cabell," she said.

I turned around to see a swirling mist of the storm in the distance, just over a small hill. Obviously, we had flown from that as if spit out of a tornado.

"That's our lifeline," Nivea said. "If we can get to that, we can reach out beyond the planet. It's a shot in the dark, but maybe we can reach someone through the storm that can help."

"Can we make it that far?" I asked.

"We have at least two hours, based on our previous smoking of the 'liefs." Fathom resolved. "Let's set out."

As we made our way up over the hill, I had to walk in

a haphazard fashion to avoid some bigger objects in the soil. Rocks? I bent down to study them.

"What is it?" Nivea asked.

"These...rocks. They actually appear to be some sort of brick. Is it possible there was a civilization here?"

Nivea came to my side and investigated the artifacts. "It's quite possible, but let's press on, we don't have too long. Keep a couple of the artifacts."

We moved up on over the hill until the storm was in view. In front of the storm, there appeared to be the outline of a deserted structure. Could this have been a building? It's long vertical elevation looked familiar. As we got closer, we could see that on the roof there was a device that looked a lot like a telescope.

"Looks like an observatory. But could it be human?" I mused.

Nivea pondered the sight. "It looks as such."

"The storm is just over there." I pointed.

"Okay," Nivea said. "Now, there's no telling what the effects will be like considering we've smoked the Ondas 'lief as well as the Marzanna 'lief. So, proceed cautiously. When you enter the storm, direct your mind to any nearby life forces you can sense, and if that doesn't work, reach out as far as you can to try to gather as much knowledge about this planet as possible."

We walked into the storm.

The storm lifted my consciousness up, up into space, although I still felt like my feet were connected to the planet. I was able to reach out into the universe.

I sought to find Earth, but I could not find it through the storm, instead I kept falling back on our current planet. Amateurism with the storm, perhaps. Nevertheless, I was bound in close proximity to my friends, and I could sense their minds exploring beside me.

Nivea, for example, was reaching out to her Breaus in Marzanna, carrying on a conversation with a Breau that must have been present in the storm there. Fathom was also searching for Earth, but also his obsession was with some other energy which didn't hold a distinguished physical shape but remained fully present.

So, I focused on where we were. I tried to map the entire planet, but it was impossible. The storm did not reach over the whole thing. I transcended the storm to recreate an image of everything it touched. There was no life, yet there seemed to be a residue of something left over, as if there had been something significant here.

As I concentrated harder, an image became more prevalent. Closed shops. Unfriendly glances. Callous, inhospitable faces. Turned away. Cold winds. The memory of a home once ripe with life now torn, thrown into an unfamiliar terrain, a void of non-existence.

Falling apart on street corners, hungry, cold, without food, without friends or family, at the precipice of a great unknown. A freezing. Cold. White. Wasteland.

Years turned to decades. Faces grew apart. Dark glances left only coldness behind, each striving to build its own barriers, mere fallible defenses against the unbeatable storm.

Alone. In the most unforgiving of conditions. What more is there to do than leave? Like footprints through the snow into the forest, what secrets could the forest hold? What other worlds could exist?

Still, there is life after leaving. Life in everything. Life in the forest. Life in the jungle. Life in the ocean. Life in the mountains. And yes, life in the storm. There is life in the storm, somehow.

The footprints flash through my mind like when we first saw him, when we first tracked him. Footprints leading into the woods, weaving through the stars, somehow the path led here, to this dead world. Somehow, it is the same. This existence, despite emptiness, it is the same.

Still, there is life.

I could feel the planet now, in my grasp. And I could sense a warmth present. A new beginning. Within us? Yes, but more. There were more voices here. Many voices, many minds, many memories, all of rejuvenation. Rebirth. Despite past failings, despite past conflicts, there would be a continuation. The forest never completely frees of the threat of fire, but after the fire, the trees grow back stronger. The world can't escape the storm, but there can be relief from it.

I could feel the others tuning in to my experience, wide-eyed with curiosity. Perhaps for the first time, I was truly glad they were there. Without them, this planet, this universe, was a desolate place. We all felt something more, something new, with the traces of what we'd be left with: A great puzzle to solve at the behest of a great explorer whose journey never ended. There was still something here that needed to continue, something of value that could be saved, something to start anew.

I fell out of the storm.

"Cabell, I saw it too," Nivea said.

"And me," Fathom said.

"It was powerful," Nivea said. "My heart felt like there was still something here from a time long ago that was nearly completely destroyed."

"Yes," I said. I paused, marinating with the new ideas. *After death, there is still life. After fire, the trees grow back stronger. The leaves grow back stronger. The… 'liefs, grow back stronger.*

"Nivea," I said. "The Atavika 'lief. What if we could keep growing it?"

Nivea paused, deep in thought. "When I was regularly connected to the storm, we maintained information in our thought archive on several planets with dire conditions. Many of these planets appeared to have no long-term sustainability for life, yet still they grew into vibrant worlds, due to the flora growing on them. Are you suggesting that the 'lief may be like the flora we found, capable of terraforming?"

"Yes," I said. "Atavika was lush with life and impenetrable from the harsh effects of the storm. What if we could replicate that on a planetary scale?"

"It's possible. We have the water from Ondas, the sun of this planet and the Atavika 'lief. And we have soil that may be tenable. But we'd have to find food to survive."

"The plant grows fast."

"At this point, anything works," said Fathom.

"It's decided then. Back to the ship," I said.

IV

We returned to the ship and spent the next few hours planting the Atavika 'lief. After a few days, the plants had grown quite large, shooting up towards space. We had tried to operate the ship multiple times, to no avail, surviving only on water collected in the ship from Ondas, and the new Atavika 'liefs that had grown.

It was looking like we would be able to sustain life here for a longer period of time than we'd initially thought, although the storm was leaving our area which meant we no longer were able to reach out to Marzanna and other planets for possible communication. We were in dire need of food.

Then, one day, we all jumped into the ship and closed the doors. I took the pilot's seat. With numerous attempts, there was a remarkable boost and, the thing jolted to life. I shivered as the ship shook and we flew through the Atavika plants now growing up towards space.

Quickly though, the launch became horrifying. My piloting skills were rough. Instead of twirling into a spiral that sent us up into space, the ship sputtered and shook left and right, nearly dropping to the ground.

We must have been fifty stories up when we took a dive downward, straight towards a peak of soil. Nivea screamed and Fathom gasped; we all braced for impact. At the last moment, before hitting the soil, I grabbed the wheel and pulled down. We cleared the peak of soil by mere inches. We pulled up over the hill safely stabilizing at a reasonable height.

As we cruised over the gray regolith, there was static sound emitting from Fathom's jacket. The two-way radio! Fathom pulled it out. A station came in clear.

"...Have we got a story for you! The *Revisit* craft has been actively exploring our Terra surface, with its intelligent robot Talus, and it's found quite a treasure this time! In the former Vancouver, now a wasteland of ash consumed by a Level 6 storm, Talus found an anti-storm respirator! Hard to imagine we once relied on these things. Astrologist Jill Fleming joins us to discuss the ramifications of this amazing discovery."

"Thank you, Olivia. Yes, it's been exhilarating to be on the team responsible for discovering the respirator. It reminds us that, in the early seventieth century, when the planet was grasping with a solution to the storm, anti-storm respirators were a temporary solution used to create a breathable atmosphere. That was foolish, of course, but it led to some interesting stories from crackpot stoners who ventured into the storm, raving of crazy planetary worlds existing beyond our planet.

"But this is the time that the concept of creating a breathable atmosphere really did gain momentum, which led to the forcefield technology we have today. Ironically, we celebrate the anniversary of this technology at a point where it has become perilously outdated, and we once again are seeking a sustainable solution to the storm."

"Thanks so very much for that brief on the respirator Jill. Now let's head to Jena for the forecast."

"Thank you, Oliva. In celebration of surviving the storm for a decade, Dome Environmental Control will be scheduling a special surprise for tomorrow: a snowstorm! Pull out your old snowsuits and prepare for a trip down nostalgia lane. This storm's gonna be a doozy!"

V

"Are we on earth?" Nivea asked, staring at me.

I stared blankly ahead as the ship continued cruising towards the horizon. "We…we can't be. This planet is desolate, uninhabitable. It can't be earth."

"But the mention of Vancouver," Fathom said. "The radio broadcast...it just sounded so real. Just like earth."

"Many worlds," Nivea said, staring at the two-way radio that was now emitting static. "The universe is vast. There are many worlds out there, many we have yet to discover. With the Marzanna 'lief, we have found and helped many simply through following mindful curiosity. It is the same mindfulness that brought us to Aras when I desired to reach Saranyu.

"It's what brought me to Kostroma, to free the Bies," said Fathom. "It's filled me with this...calm."

"It wouldn't be possible without this ship," said Nivea. "It truly is...a gift. From Hylotz. What did you want when you took the wheel, Cabell?"

"The same thing I've always wanted. A solution to the storm. To save earth. To find Hylotz. But beyond that, I guess I wanted to connect. To find others that recognize that common goal. To *feel* life, rather than just research about it. And, of course, I wanted us all to return home."

As I finished speaking, a structure appeared on the horizon. It took a few moments more before we realized what it was. It was a forcefield dome. The radio signal was correct, there was life here.

We cheered as I guided the ship towards the force-field, when suddenly the two-way radio jolted to life with an intermittent flickering voice.

"This is Dome Defense, come in, over."

We glanced at each other in excitement. Fathom took up the two-way radio.

"Roger, this is Fathom."

"Please identify yourself and explain exactly where you

have come from and how you got here."

Each of us looked at the other in disbelief.

"We…are from Earth. We found this ship, and…it's a long story."

"We have detected three humans in your unidentified space-craft. Do you represent a stranded faction of survivors of the storm?"

"We are survivors of the storm, but when we left Earth, we left it in a much different condition than this planet."

"This planet is Earth. Are you suggesting you are from a different planet?"

Again, we looked at each other.

"We don't know," said Fathom. "We just know that this is not the Earth we remember. The Earth we left, not long ago, was dying in a storm."

"It has been decades since we found a tenable solution to the storm," said the voice. *"…albeit a fallible one. Your ship is entirely foreign. It is as if you have fallen out of another world. Regardless, we welcome you and we hope to learn more of your origins."*

I reached for the two-way communicator.

"I just have one important question for you," I said. "Where is your nearest washroom?"

ABOUT THE AUTHOR

Andrew Pike is from St. John's, holding a degree in English from Memorial University of Newfoundland, as well as diplomas in Journalism and Music from College of the North Atlantic.

He nurtures an unhealthy addiction to coffee, has written for *The Telegram*, and plays classical piano.

Previously published stories include 'Escape from Selenous Valley Retreat' in *Dystopia from the Rock* and 'Slipdream' from *Pulp Science-Fiction from the Rock*.

The Epic Quest For Terral B. Hylotz is his first novel.